John Creasey – Mas

Born in Surrey, England in 1908 int
were nine children, John Creasey grew up to be a true master story teller and international sensation. His more than 600 crime, mystery and thriller titles have now sold 80 million copies in 25 languages. These include many popular series such as *Gideon of Scotland Yard*, *The Toff*, *Dr Palfrey* and *The Baron*.

Creasy wrote under many pseudonyms, explaining that booksellers had complained he totally dominated the 'C' section in stores. They included:

Gordon Ashe, M E Cooke, Norman Deane, Robert Caine Frazer, Patrick Gill, Michael Halliday, Charles Hogarth, Brian Hope, Colin Hughes, Kyle Hunt, Abel Mann, Peter Manton, J J Marric, Richard Martin, Rodney Mattheson, Anthony Morton and *Jeremy York*.

Never one to sit still, Creasey had a strong social conscience, and stood for Parliament several times, along with founding the One Party Alliance which promoted the idea of government by a coalition of the best minds from across the political spectrum.

He also founded the British Crime Writers' Association, which to this day celebrates outstanding crime writing. The Mystery Writers of America bestowed upon him the Edgar Award for best novel and then in 1969 the ultimate Grand Master Award. John Creasey's stories are as compelling today as ever.

INPECTOR WEST SERIES

INSPECTOR WEST TAKES CHARGE
INSPECTOR WEST LEAVES TOWN (ALSO PUBLISHED AS: GO AWAY TO MURDER)
INSPECTOR WEST AT HOME (ALSO PUBLISHED AS: AN APOSTLE OF GLOOM)
INSPECTOR WEST REGRETS
HOLIDAY FOR INSPECTOR WEST
BATTLE FOR INSPECTOR WEST
TRIUMPH FOR INSPECTOR WEST (ALSO PUBLISHED AS: THE CASE AGAINST PAUL RAEBURN)
INSPECTOR WEST KICKS OFF (ALSO PUBLISHED AS: SPORT FOR INSPECTOR WEST)
INSPECTOR WEST ALONE
INSPECTOR WEST CRIES WOLF (ALSO PUBLISHED AS: THE CREEPERS)
A CASE FOR INSPECTOR WEST (ALSO PUBLISHED AS: THE FIGURE IN THE DUSK)
PUZZLE FOR INSPECTOR WEST (ALSO PUBLISHED AS: THE DISSEMBLERS)
INSPECTOR WEST AT BAY (ALSO PUBLISHED AS: THE CASE OF THE ACID THROWERS)
A GUN FOR INSPECTOR WEST (ALSO PUBLISHED AS: GIVE A MAN A GUN)
SEND INSPECTOR WEST (ALSO PUBLISHED AS: SEND SUPERINTENDENT WEST)
A BEAUTY FOR INSPECTOR WEST (ALSO PUBLISHED AS: THE BEAUTY QUEEN KILLER)
INSPECTOR WEST MAKES HASTE (ALSO PUBLISHED AS: MURDER MAKES HASTE)
TWO FOR INSPECTOR WEST (ALSO PUBLISHED AS: MURDER: ONE, TWO, THREE)
PARCELS FOR INSPECTOR WEST (ALSO PUBLISHED AS: DEATH OF A POSTMAN)
A PRINCE FOR INSPECTOR WEST (ALSO PUBLISHED AS: DEATH OF A ASSASSIN)
ACCIDENT FOR INSPECTOR WEST (ALSO PUBLISHED AS: HIT AND RUN)
FIND INSPECTOR WEST (ALSO PUBLISHED AS: DOORWAY TO DEATH)
MURDER, LONDON - NEW YORK
STRIKE FOR DEATH (ALSO PUBLISHED AS: THE KILLING STRIKE)
DEATH OF A RACEHORSE
THE CASE OF THE INNOCENT VICTIMS
MURDER ON THE LINE
DEATH IN COLD PRINT
THE SCENE OF THE CRIME
POLICEMAN'S DREAD
HANG THE LITTLE MAN
LOOK THREE WAYS AT MURDER
MURDER, LONDON - AUSTRALIA
MURDER, LONDON - SOUTH AFRICA
THE EXECUTIONERS
SO YOUNG TO BURN
MURDER, LONDON - MIAMI
A PART FOR A POLICEMAN
ALIBI (ALSO PUBLISHED AS: ALIBI FOR INSPECTOR WEST)
A SPLINTER OF GLASS
THE THEFT OF MAGNA CARTA
THE EXTORTIONERS
A SHARP RISE IN CRIME

The Case of the Innocent Victims

John Creasey

Copyright © 1959 John Creasey Literary management Ltd.
© 2014 House of Stratus

All rights reserved. No part of this publication may be reproduced, stored in a retrieval system, or transmitted, in any form, or by any means (electronic, mechanical, photocopying, recording, or otherwise), without the prior permission of the publisher. Any person who does any unauthorised act in relation to this publication may be liable to criminal prosecution and civil claims for damages.

The right of John Creasey to be identified as the author of this work has been asserted.

This edition published in 2014 by House of Stratus, an imprint of
Stratus Books Ltd., Lisandra House, Fore Street,
Looe, Cornwall, PL13 1AD, U.K.
www.houseofstratus.com

Typeset by House of Stratus.

A catalogue record for this book is available from the British Library and the Library of Congress.

ISBN 07551-3535-0
EAN 978-07551-3535-6

This book is sold subject to the condition that it shall not be lent, resold, hired out, or otherwise circulated without the publisher's express prior consent in any form of binding, or cover, other than the original as herein published and without a similar condition being imposed on any subsequent purchaser, or bona fide possessor.

This is a fictional work and all characters are drawn from the author's imagination.
Any resemblance or similarities to persons either living or dead are entirely coincidental.

Chapter One

Woman in Despair

"Mad or not," Gibson said, "I'd string 'em up. And you needn't give me any of that 'our job's to catch 'em, not to worry about what happens to them afterwards'. First I'd give them the cat, and then I'd string 'em up."

Superintendent Roger West was walking beside him, along a narrow street which led to Bank Terrace. It was quicker to go this way, leaving Roger's car behind them, than to drive right up to the house. A crowd had already gathered; newspapermen were there in their dozens; and probably there was an ambulance, certainly several Divisional police cars.

The footsteps of the two large men echoed. It was dark overhead, but the fluorescent lamplight was good, so that these men of the Criminal Investigation Department at New Scotland Yard could see each other clearly. Roger, an inch the taller and perhaps an inch the broader, did not actually smile; his lips curved in a sardonic way which Gibson was getting to know well.

"I don't care how much you blow off steam with me," he said mildly, "but don't let the newspaper chaps hear you talk like that."

"Probably every one of them will be screaming what I'm saying from the headlines," Gibson retorted.

"Let 'em – so long as they don't quote a copper," Roger said.

Just ahead was a policeman, quite short in spite of his helmet. He was blocking the path, and shone his flashlight into their faces as if to make quite sure who they were.

"Superintendent West?"

"Yes."

"This way, sir."

"Thanks," Roger said.

They stepped through a narrow gateway into a small, narrow garden. Ahead of them was the back of the long terrace of tall houses, with oblongs of light showing many windows. At the house to which the garden belonged every window was ablaze with light, and shadows moved against the curtains of one on the second floor.

"There's another officer on duty at the back door, sir," their guide said.

"Thanks." Roger nodded, and led the way – but as he saw the pale light which showed the silhouette of a policeman against an open door, the quiet was pierced by a sharp, high-pitched scream.

The sound went through Roger; involuntarily, he stopped. Gibson bumped into him. They stared up at the window where the shadows were, and suddenly these became much darker. The shape of a woman appeared against the bottom pane, there was a squeak of sound, and the window shot up.

A woman appeared.

There was just enough light to reveal her face, but not to see the awful expression on it; that was left to the men's imagination. She was screaming, as if her mouth were wide open and she could not stop. For a moment it looked as if she would throw herself out.

"Why the hell doesn't someone stop her?" Gibson exclaimed.

Another shadow appeared against the window. The woman seemed to be struggling, and her screaming fell away to a gasping sound. The hands and the arms of a man they could not see were at her shoulders, restraining her.

"All right," Roger said, and turned towards the back door.

"First left, and then right, sir," the second constable said.

"Thanks. How long has this been going on?"

"Twenty minutes or so, sir, on and off."

"Know the woman – what's her name?"

"Mrs Kindle, sir. I don't exactly know her, but I've often seen her, wheeling the—" The man broke off.

"Hmm," said Roger. "So this is your beat?"

"Yes, sir."

"I'll want a full report on everything you know about Mrs Kindle, her neighbours, husband, friends – the lot," Roger said. "Tell the chap at the garden gate, will you? And put it round the station. Some of you may be having a late night."

"If it would help to get the devil who did that job, we'd work all night for a month."

"Sure you would," said Roger, and nodded.

He stepped into the kitchen of the ground-floor flat in the house, which had four floors and four flats altogether. There was a faint smell of cooking, a little stale but not really unpleasant, and there was also a slight smell of gas. A light shone in a passage which led to the left, and another uniformed policeman stood at the foot of a flight of stairs. The front door, leading to the crowds, was shut, and doubtless other men were on duty on the porch, to make sure that no one could slip through. The only sound seemed to be that of a woman, crying. In the bright landing light, Gibson was looking pale and angry. That didn't matter, provided it did not destroy his judgment. He had been recently promoted to Chief Inspector's rank at the Yard, and had come originally from this Division – AS. That was why Roger had brought him on this investigation. Gibson was in the early forties, and last year his fourth son had been born. In the same year, his second son had died; it wasn't surprising that Gibson felt keenly about the suffering of the woman upstairs.

For her child, her infant son, had died only a few hours ago.

Finding the murderer was only one problem; one to flash across the headlines of the newspapers, to rumble about the Yard, to be tapped along the teletype machines and winged along the wires – all these noises gradually becoming fainter until the horror of this night was forgotten except in the heart and the mind of the mother, and perhaps of the father, who was away at sea.

The mother would have to face the greater part of this burden on her own.

Gibson also knew that.

It was a good thing for a detective to have a soft spot, to feel keenly, to hate the men he was after, but a bad thing if it warped his judgment or influenced his actions. Although this case would reach its peak soon, and then gradually fade, its influences on Gibson might last for a long time, and so affect the dozens of cases he would investigate every year, the hundreds in the course of his service at the Yard. It was important to try to help this mother, and to find the killer of a four-month old baby; it was vital to put Gibson right if he showed signs of going wrong.

They went up a flight of narrow stairs, Roger in the lead. The door of a flat was closed and there was no light at the sides. There was plenty of light above their heads, for the front door of the bereaved woman's flat was open. As Roger and Gibson reached the landing, they saw two uniformed policemen and, beyond, three plain-clothes men. One of them was on his knees and using, of all things, a large magnifying glass. The crying was coming from a room beyond.

A thickset man of medium height came hurrying from there. He had a chunky face, very light blue eyes, and a briskness and lightness of tread which was somehow surprising. He wore a well-cut and well-pressed suit of pale grey; his iron-grey hair was cut very close. He thrust out his hand, and said: "You didn't lose any time."

"Tried not to," Roger said, and looked towards the door of the room from which the man had come. "Has she seen a doctor?"

"Going to have a sedative in five minutes," the other said, and nodded to Gibson. "Hallo, Gibby, hope you don't try to run the Yard as you tried to run AS." There was no spite in the words. "Before you see the mother, Handsome, there are one or two little things it might be helpful to know. Her husband's somewhere off the coast of South America, and even if he were allowed to fly back from the nearest port, it would be several days before he could get here. And there's another man in her life. According to what I've been able to find out from neighbours, this other chap wants her to get a divorce, but she refuses because of the baby."

"My God!" exclaimed Gibson.

"Handsome will soon start telling you not to jump to conclusions, so I'll say it for him," the thickset man said. He was Ledbetter, the Superintendent of the Division. "That's why I've kept questioning her a bit, tried to find out if this other fellow had been around tonight."

"Has he?"

"She just goes into hysterics every time I ask."

"Better give her a rest," Roger advised. "Sent someone for this chap?"

"Haven't got his address yet; we only picked up the information from a neighbour," Ledbetter answered. "But we're digging."

"Go deep," said Roger dryly.

All policemen, even leading members of the Criminal Investigation Department, could be classified, and Ledbetter's classification was 'hard'. He would conduct an investigation and deal with witnesses coldly and harshly, and almost to a point of cruelty. He knew that this was never approved, and had learned to make excuses for any apparent excesses. In fact, he didn't go over the line into third degree, and apart from the one hard streak, he was genial and easy to get along with.

He had been forcing his questions too hard on the mother, believing that if he kept the pressure up long and severely enough, he would make her break down and talk of anything she knew. That might even be justified, if she knew anything to help.

Roger went into the next room.

This was the living-room, with its window, closed now, overlooking the back garden. The curtains were thrust to one side, as they had been when Roger had seen what had happened. Two detectives and a small man were in the room; the small man was almost certainly the doctor. Roger didn't recognise him. He was a striking-looking man, sharp-featured, with dark, glossy hair; and he looked annoyed.

The mother was sitting in a chair, silent now, head resting on the back of the chair, hands clutching the arms, eyes closed. Tears were trickling down her cheeks. Her eyes were red and puffy, her face blotchy, and yet in spite of all that, her good looks showed through. Her hair was fair and fluffy, and looked as if she had just combed and brushed it. She was breathing hard through her parted lips, and quivering a little.

She had quite a figure, and a pale-blue twin set was stretched tight across her thrusting bosom.

The little man asked abruptly: "Are you Superintendent West?"

"Yes, sir."

"I've been as patient as I can be," the man said sharply. "I am Dr Frascatti, and I was asked not to give Mrs Kindle a sedative until you'd had a chance to speak to her. But I cannot allow any further questioning, no matter how well-intentioned or how necessary you regard it."

Ledbetter had really rubbed him up the wrong way.

"I needn't be two minutes," Roger said placatingly. "If this were the only case of its kind we wouldn't have pushed so hard, but it's the second in a week, Dr Frascatti, and—"

"You cannot bring the children back."

"If we find the right man we might save a third," Roger answered mildly, and Frascatti seemed momentarily abashed. The woman had not opened her eyes, and had taken no notice of Roger. She didn't when he turned to her and said: "Mrs Kindle, will you give us the address of your friend, Mr Cartwright?"

She did not answer, and did not open her eyes. Frascatti had opened a small box from his case, and was taking out a hypodermic syringe. A small bottle with a sealed top stood close to his bag. In a minute, he would have the syringe loaded, and would jab; a few minutes after that the woman would get a respite from her grief; but only a respite.

"Mrs Kindle," Roger said matter-of-factly, "would you like us to get into radio communication with your husband, and have him fly home?"

Mrs Kindle's eyes opened so quickly that it was startling. They were big and blue, wet with tears and dull with shock, but a glint showed in them as she exclaimed: "No!"

"We could arrange it, if you like."

"No!" she cried. "No, don't fetch John. Don't fetch him, he—"

"All right, Mrs Kindle. What did you say Mr Cartwright's address was?"

She stared at him, the glint fading from her eyes and the dullness coming back. She did not close her eyes again, but obviously she did not intend to say a word. Ledbetter had a half grin, a kind of 'I-told-you-so' look about him. The doctor held the syringe poised. Roger stood back and motioned to him, and watched as he pushed up the sleeve of Mrs Kindle's left arm.

"This won't hurt, Mrs Kindle," Frascatti soothed. "Just a slight prick, that's all, and you'll be asleep within a few minutes." He rubbed spirit on to the fleshy part of the arm just above the elbow, and jabbed; he was swift and competent, and the woman hardly flinched. "That's all you have to worry about," he reassured her, and there was an expression almost of triumph in his face when he looked at Ledbetter.

The woman closed her eyes.

It was easier to understand Ledbetter's attitude now, and even to share his feeling that the woman knew more about the murder of the child than anyone would like to think. But it was too late to take advantage of that; it had been when Roger had arrived.

Before he could turn away, there came a sound of heavy footsteps on the stairs, including those of a man running with swift, urgent steps; no policeman was likely to show such wild haste. Roger turned towards the door and, as he did so, saw the woman's eyes open wide, saw the way she gripped the arms of her chair and tried to get up. In a few seconds she would be unconscious, and she knew it; but in this moment she did not want the promised respite, and her eyes were glaring.

A man said heavily: "I'm sorry, sir, you can't go any further. If you'll give me your name I'll ask the Superintendent."

"Then hurry, don't just stand there," a man ordered hotly. "My name's Cartwright, I'm a friend of Mrs Kindle. And I want to know what's happened. I insist on knowing."

Ledbetter looked startled, too, and Mrs Kindle's expression was one of real alarm. But she could not get up, and the doctor held one shoulder, Gibson the other, to restrain her. Roger reached the door in two strides, and called: "Let Mr Cartwright come in."

A policeman stood aside hastily. Cartwright, who was at the foot of the flight of steps immediately below the landing, came running up; a tall, nice-looking lad – lad was the word which occurred to Roger. His hair was unruly, his collar and tie looked as if they had been hurriedly fastened.

Roger stood aside, and then watched the face of Cartwright and the woman as they set eyes on each other.

Chapter Two

Guilt?

The difficulty was to watch them both; but the woman's expression seemed to freeze, and did not change from moment to moment. The man's did. He stopped moving, when he saw Mrs Kindle. He formed a name: "Anne," but it was little more than a whisper, and he gave the impression that he was choking. At first he looked terribly concerned, but now shock touched his eyes, perhaps bewilderment, too, and even horror. He didn't move.

Anne Kindle tried to moisten her lips, but it seemed as if she could not. Her eyes were so heavy that they actually closed once, and she forced them open again; Frascatti's injection really carried a punch. She no longer made any attempt to get out of her chair, and Gibson took his hand away from her shoulder.

Then Cartwright moved again.

"Anne, it—it can't be true," he said, and reached her and went down on his right knee in front of her. "Anne, don't look at me like that. Anne!"

She had stopped looking at him, for her eyes were glazing over. Given a minute's foreknowledge, Roger could have forestalled that injection and so won the full benefit of this encounter, but he had given way where Ledbetter would have held out; and no one could be surprised if Ledbetter felt that his own tactics had been wiser.

They all made a kind of tableau, which had to be broken soon. Roger broke it, moving towards the chair and the unconscious woman, and saying quite briskly: "Will you need a nurse, doctor?"

"Someone will have to stay with her; she mustn't be alone when she comes round," Frascatti answered.

"According to her neighbours, she hasn't any relatives near," Ledbetter declared.

"Better get her to a nursing home," Roger said. "Will you fix it, Percy?" He spoke to Ledbetter, who nodded; he would arrange for the woman to go to a small nursing home in the Division, where she could be watched all the time; it would be necessary to have someone by her bedside, to take a statement when she came round. All of those things were routine, and no further word was necessary. "Mr Cartwright," Roger went on, looking at the back of Cartwright's head, "I'd like you to tell us why you came here tonight."

Cartwright was almost as motionless as the woman he called Anne, but he began to get up, slowly and laboriously. He was a nice-looking 'lad'; that word came to Roger's mind again. He had fine grown eyes, long lashes, and a perfect complexion, the kind that a woman would dream about. Was he slightly effeminate? He was tall and carelessly dressed, giving the impression that he did not have much dress sense. He glanced round at Roger, but obviously had no desire to look away from Mrs Kindle.

Ledbetter gave a word of instruction to a man just outside, Frascatti was putting away his hypodermic syringe, and had a rather smug look. Gibson showed that gift which had helped him to get where he was; of being part of the background, without intruding at all.

"I—I was told that Anne's – that her baby had been murdered." He pressed a hand across his forehead, as if his head were aching badly, and went on, slowly: "I couldn't believe it."

"Who told you?"

"I had a telephone call."

"Who from?"

"A woman who said she lived near here, a neighbour," Cartwright answered.

"Do you know her name?"

"No, what the hell does her name matter? I rushed straight here to find out if it were true. I can—I can hardly believe—"

"Have you been here before tonight?" Roger interrupted.

"I just can't believe—"

"Answer my questions at once, please," Roger said, more in the Ledbetter tradition. "Have you been here before, tonight?"

Cartwright muttered: "I—I did just look in, yes."

"Have you been inside this flat before, tonight?"

"Yes."

"When?"

"I—I'm not sure of the exact time."

"Tell us as nearly as you can."

"About—about eight o'clock, I suppose," Cartwright replied, and his voice strengthened a little, although the scared look remained. "I hoped that Anne would—would come out for the evening, but she couldn't get a sitter-in. So I—I left."

"Did you leave Mrs Kindle on good terms?"

Cartwright looked away.

"Did you leave her on good terms or did you have a quarrel?" demanded Roger harshly.

Ledbetter was actually nodding approval.

Cartwright said furiously: "Why are you shouting at me like that? My God, do you think I know anything about—" He broke off, staring at the unconscious woman. She was leaning forward a little, her whole body drooping. Men were approaching in the street, but whoever was in charge outside would keep them away during these vital moments. "I know nothing about it. I—good God, I wouldn't hurt a fly! And as for Nigel—" He moistened his lips and looked round at the other men present, as if he were afraid of the accusation and the condemnation in the eyes of the men watching him. "What's happened to everybody?" he demanded, almost wildly. "Why did Anne look at me like that?"

"Did you, or did you not, quarrel with Mrs Kindle?" Roger demanded sharply.

"We—we had a few words, that's all."

"So you quarrelled."

"It—it wasn't really a quarrel. I—I told her that she was making a slave of herself for the child, and that it was—" He broke off.

"It was what?"

"It—it was time her husband took his share of the responsibility," Cartwright said, in a low-pitched voice. "And that's true enough, but I didn't harm the baby. Yet the way she looked at me …" His voice quavered and rose, then dropped away, as if he had been shocked beyond endurance. He looked pale and ill, too, muttered what might have been: "It doesn't make any sense," and walked to the side of the room, pressing a hand against his forehead.

Roger signalled to Ledbetter, who was at the door. An ambulance man came in, with a plain-clothes Divisional man, carrying a stretcher; that was the easy way to take Mrs Kindle out of the flat. Cartwright turned to watch, his eyes glittering as if with both pain and distress. He made a move towards Mrs Kindle as the two men lifted the stretcher, but then held back. Roger, watching him closely, knew that Gibson and Ledbetter missed nothing. Outside, the Divisional men were still searching for anything at all which might help them to prove the identity of the murderer.

Was Cartwright the man?

Ledbetter's money was probably on him. How old was he? Only in the early twenties, Roger judged, just before he spoke again.

"Mr Cartwright."

"Yes?"

"Can you remember the exact words of the quarrel you had with Mrs Kindle tonight?"

"I've told you that it wasn't a quarrel!"

"Can you give the exact words?"

"More or less, I suppose, but—"

"Have you quarrelled with her before?"

"Not—not really."

"Have you argued about the same subject before?"

"Yes."

"Are you in love with Mrs Kindle?"

Cartwright raised his head and looked at Roger straightly, as if with a kind of pride. He seemed to square his shoulders and to stand more erect, too.

"Yes, I am," he answered. "And I know exactly what the neighbours think, and the kind of scandal that you are going to hear. Well, it isn't true. I'm in love with Anne, but that's all there is to it. We've never"—he hesitated, and then went on rather more quickly—"given her husband cause for divorce. Anne was too loyal to him. I believe that he goes off on these long voyages simply because he doesn't want to be tied down to any one place or any one woman, but that didn't make any difference to Anne. You can discount whatever you hear about that. It won't be true."

He said all that very well. Yet there was Ledbetter, smiling and sceptical, and Gibson, somehow in the background, and showing no reaction of any kind. Cartwright was standing upright and very tall; he must be nearly six feet.

"How did you hear about the murder of the baby?" Roger demanded.

"I've told you – a woman telephoned me."

"Did she give her name?"

"I've told you that, too – no."

"Didn't you recognise her voice?"

"No, I didn't," answered Cartwright flatly. "I picked up the receiver, and she seemed to be out of breath. She said that Nigel had been murdered, and I ought to go and try to help Mrs Kindle. Then—"

"Did she say Mrs Kindle, or Anne?"

"Mrs Kindle."

"When was this?"

"Half an hour or so ago – I don't know exactly," Cartwright answered impatiently. "I live in Ealing, and came straight here. My car was jammed between two others and I was a hell of a time getting out, so I suppose it was nearer three-quarters of an hour ago. That's everything I can tell you, absolutely everything."

"Has Mrs Kindle ever suggested that she was nervous living here alone?"

"No."

"Has anyone ever threatened the child, to your knowledge?"

"No."

"Do you know Mr Kindle?"

Cartwright actually flushed. "I've met him once or twice, casually, that's all. Anne used to work at my—at the same place as I, and I met Kindle before they were married. She kept her job on until the baby came." He closed his eyes, and went on in a low-pitched voice, as if he were fighting to conceal his anguish: "She worshipped Nigel. God knows what will happen to her now, it'll drive her mad. She worshipped him, and—" He broke off, with a little choking sound, but Roger did not interrupt, and the others also watched in silence. "She believed that Nigel would bring her husband home. She thought it would make all the difference to them. There never was a chance, he's such a selfish devil, but she believed it."

Cartwright broke off again.

Roger said: "Mr. Cartwright, I would like you to make a statement repeating all you've told me, and recalling the exact words of your difference of opinion with Mrs Kindle, I'll arrange for you to go into a neighbour's room. In the morning we shall ask you to read the statement through and, if you agree that it's correct, sign it. Have you any objection?"

"No," Cartwright said, and then gulped. "No, of course not. But how will that help to find the murderer?"

"The most unexpected facts often help to do that," Roger said dryly.

Ledbetter had beckoned to a man, who came in and took instructions; a room had already been made available in the ground-floor flat. Roger watched Cartwright going off, and wasn't surprised when Ledbetter spoke as soon as the man was out of earshot: "A nice piece of acting."

"Think so?" asked Roger.

"Don't say it fooled you?" Ledbetter scoffed. "Cartwright knew that we would hear about the quarrel, and knew it was no use keeping out of sight, so he did the obvious thing – came and brazened it out. You can't need any telling that the woman thought he did it: she practically accused him as soon as she set eyes on him." Ledbetter hotted up and his voice grew harsher when Roger gave him no encouragement. "That's why she wouldn't give his name and address. She knew who the killer was the moment she realised what had happened. No wonder she went off into screaming hysteria. This is one of the quickies, Handsome."

"Could be," Roger conceded, and rubbed the tip of his nose. Unexpectedly he grinned, and that lit up his face, so that he fully justified the familiar nickname. His fair hair was wavy, and the grey in it hardly showed; he looked no more than in the middle thirties, although he was now a senior officer at the Yard, and in the middle forties. His grey eyes glinted as if he expected Ledbetter to do battle. "Supposing I leave the chores to you, and we go over them in the morning. If it's cut and dried, there's no need for me to waste my beauty sleep."

Ledbetter looked at him suspiciously: "What's on your mind?"

"Isn't it obvious?" Gibson asked unexpectedly. "Cartwright might have had reason to hate this kid, and if he lost his temper he might even have choked the life out of it. But as far as we know he didn't have any motive for killing the Shaw baby last week, did he? We'll have to find out if he had the opportunity. The killing was done the same way, wasn't it? Baby suffocated in its own cot, with its own pillow. It looks to me as if the same man did each job, or one imitated the first man's method."

Ledbetter watched Gibson throughout all this, and then said without the slightest rancour: "Tell you what, Handsome, stay and do the job with us. You might spot something we'll miss. If Gibby's right and this is the second job by the same man, then there might be others. Don't want to take any chances of concentrating on the wrong chap. You staying?"

"You try to keep me away," Roger said, and although he was smiling, there was a glint in his eyes. "Two baby murders in seven days is two too many. You know how contagious these things seem to get. Now, where's this cot?"

"Wouldn't care to have a word with the newspaper chaps before we start, would you?" Ledbetter suggested. "I don't know how they do it, but they know you're here."

"Can't you see 'em?"

"You're the glamour boy."

"What line have you taken with them so far?" Roger asked. 'Glamour boy' from some would be a taunt; from Ledbetter it was simply fair comment.

"Just told 'em to wait."

"You'd better come with me," Roger said. "Gibson, get out that report on the Shaw baby murder last week, and compare it item by item with this one." He spoke as he moved, with a kind of restrained briskness, as if he could not wait to get busy.

On the right was a small room, crowded with men; in here was a blue cot, on the walls were pictures of teddy bears and rabbits, of birds and puppies and kittens. A light flashed. He caught a glimpse of a shawl on the floor, with a chalk mark round it, as he went past, leading the way downstairs.

At least the mother was quiet and resting now.

The next job, probably the key one, was to talk to the Press. This was a case where the newspapers would take guidance, if they were offered the right angle for them. Certainly he did not want a big scare. Within a few miles of this spot there must be a thousand young mothers and a thousand infants in arms. Next morning, each mother would know fear even when they read the bare outline of the case.

If a psychopath were running loose, they would have plenty of cause for fear.

Should he say just enough to let them think that this baby's killer was already caught, even though that would be putting the public good against the individual's. But would it really be to the public good? If there were a killer on the prowl, every parent should be encouraged to take excessive care, and so make sure all young babies were closely guarded.

"What's on your mind?" Ledbetter asked as they neared the closed front door. There was a background of noise, as of many people talking, of engines running and of people walking.

"Can you remember a case like this where two have been attacked on the same night?" Roger inquired.

"No," answered the Divisional man promptly.

"Thanks," said Roger, and opened the door to a sea of faces, to sudden silence and, abruptly, to the flashing of photographers' lights.

Chapter Three

Tactics

Most of the reporters, and there were a dozen or more, were crowded to the right of the front door, flanked by two uniformed policemen who were there to send onlookers into the road, which was virtually blocked. The flashlights showed the faces of the men and two women in the group, as well as lighting up the hundreds of others, glinting on startled eyes, shining on faces which looked ghostly white. Someone near the front of the crowd called out: "There's Handsome West!"

Roger ignored that, and crossed to the newspaper reporters; the years had taught him the unwisdom of being brusque or awkward with them. He gave a quick, businesslike smile, particularly for a tall, lean man, Spendlove, of the *Globe* which had a four-million daily circulation; there was a tendency for the popular newspapers to follow the *Globe's* line if they had no axe to grind of their own.

"Got anything for us, Superintendent?" a man asked.

"Can you tell us how the child was killed?" inquired a short, dumpy woman wearing a scarf wound round her neck and flung carelessly over her right shoulder. She was Martha Wise, known as Aunt Martha, and nearly as influential as Spendlove. Her bobbed, iron-grey hair was bare, and she looked rather like an untidy Ledbetter.

"Made no arrest yet?" asked Spendlove.

Roger hesitated, looked at him, and then said slowly and as if there was some uncertainty: "No, we haven't." Then almost at once he went on more quickly, as if to cover a tactical error. "The baby was suffocated with its own pillow. There's no doubt about that. It must have been over in a few seconds. No injuries except faint swelling of the lips, caused by pressure. So you needn't run the beast-on-the-prowl line." He flashed his grin again. "And if any of you quote me, I'll never talk to a reporter again! Just quote some anonymous policeman."

Spendlove said: "All right, Handsome. Any known connection with the Shaw baby murder last week?"

Roger was decisive.

"None that we know of, except that the same method was used, and that doesn't necessarily mean much. Imitative crimes are pretty common. We're checking, of course, but so far we haven't had any indication that the same man did both jobs."

"So you really think you've got the chap for this one?" said Spendlove, and the others were obviously willing to let him act as spokesman. "Who is it? This woman's lover?"

"Lover?" echoed Roger.

Spendlove grinned. "Don't play innocent, Handsome. The chap who came bursting in just now but hasn't come bursting out. He's the boy friend. The neighbours told us that – name of Cartwright, too. In fact I could tell you the name of the neighbour who found him in the telephone book and phoned him to come. She thought it only right that he should come to the help of his distressed paramour! Did he kill the baby?"

"He's making a statement," Roger said. "Don't push me too hard."

"Anything about the husband?" asked the grey-haired woman. "Are you going to try to get him back from South America?"

"Not up to me to decide, but I shouldn't think so," Roger said. "He can't help us in our inquiries. If the woman's advisers think it will help they'll tell the shipping company, and it will be up to them. Probably depend on how near port the husband's ship is. We're not likely to make any request. What's the name of this neighbour, did you say?"

Spendlove grinned. "I didn't say. She's Mrs Harris, next door but one. Thanks, Handsome." He turned away, to get to the nearest telephone, and the other reporters seemed to vanish, each to the private house where he had arranged to use the telephone, or to the kiosks round the corner, or to radio-equipped cars. It was done, and Roger turned back into the house.

Ledbetter was giving a toothy smile.

"Crafty old so-and-so," he said.

"How about asking Mrs Harris if she'll come in for a few minutes," Roger suggested. "I'd like to know what she can tell us, she obviously knew more about Cartwright than the other neighbours. Will you fix it?"

"Right away," promised Ledbetter.

Mrs Harris was a small, youngish woman, with a sense of mission. Every other sentence she used began with 'It was only right'. It was only right that Cartwright should be told, it was only right that the newspapers should know the truth, it was only right that everyone with young babies should be protected. Roger came to the conclusion that she could not help at all. She was nearer Anne Kindle's age than anyone else who lived nearby, and had toddlers of her own. Now and again Anne had confided in her about Cartwright, it seemed, and she knew his Christian name and the district he lived in, so she had found it easy to find his telephone number.

"And it's only right to say that she assured me there was nothing *wrong;* she wouldn't allow anything like that. But I must say I could understand it if she had kicked over the traces. That husband of hers isn't worth his own signature, that's what I say. Here today, gone tomorrow, all the time; I'll bet he's never been faithful to her like she has to him. But he ought to be sent for, that's what I say. It's only right that a husband should stand by his wife in time of trouble."

"Did you see Mr Cartwright here tonight, Mrs Harris?"

"Only the second time. I didn't know about the first time until my husband told me he'd seen him. But it wouldn't have made any difference, I would have telephoned him anyhow. It was only right …"

When she had gone, Roger went upstairs to compare the notes which Gibson had made. The routine of the investigation was nearly done. One or two men stood about idly, one yawning, and Roger saw where they had used fingerprint powder to bring up prints for photographing them. He also saw the signs which showed that the windows had been examined closely and every square inch of floor and wall searched, both in the child's room and in the passage leading to it, as well as on the staircase. Other rooms in the flat had been examined, but more cursorily. Roger sat against a table in the living-room, looking at the notes Gibson had made, and Ledbetter was squinting at them from one side.

"The baby was about the same age, a boy, only child, sleeping alone in a room in a flat, and suffocated with its own pillow," Roger said at last. "No other similarities as far as we can tell."

"That's plenty," observed Ledbetter dryly.

"Could be."

"The two murders took place within ten minutes' walk of each other," Gibson pointed out.

"Ah," said Roger. "Point I'd overlooked." He grinned at Ledbetter. "Nice job to have in your Division, I'll bet you don't get much sleep for a week. Know what I'd do, if I were you?"

"Tell me."

"Check every household in the Division where there's a child of this age, so that we know the exact tally. Tell all the chaps on the beat to keep a special eye on the places. I'll arrange for the neighbouring Divisions to keep a lookout close to yours," Roger went on. "We'll get the whole thing planned as if we knew that the devil was going to strike again any night now. Okay?"

"Yes. How about Cartwright? Going to let him go?"

"Yes. Like us to have a man follow him, or will you do that?"

"I'd like it to be one of your chaps, as he's outside the Division," Ledbetter said.

He was really saying that he did not think he had a man reliable enough to do a good tailing job, Roger knew. The Divisions seemed to have good and bad patches in certain ways; AS lacked good tailers.

"I'll fix it," he promised. "You got a note of Cartwright's address, Gibby?"

"Yes."

"Fine. I'm going to question him again, but I won't take him to the Yard yet. If he's scared he might do something silly, such as try to run away. That would give us another angle. What time was this job done – can we be sure?"

"No. But the baby was alive at eight and dead by a quarter to ten."

"What about the Shaw job?"

"Same kind of timing."

"Hm. Let's have Cartwright in again."

The man who was in love with Anne Kindle was now much more composed, and less disposed to be difficult; danger often had a quietening effect on the quick-tempered, in Roger's experience. He answered the same questions quietly, giving the same answers, and hesitated only when Roger asked: "Can you tell me where you were last Friday evening, Mr Cartwright?"

"Friday?" Cartwright frowned. "Er—well, nowhere special. I like to get off for the weekend if I'm going away, but last Friday I was home all the evening, I think. Why?"

So he had no alibi for the Shaw murder.

"Do you know a Mr and Mrs Shaw?"

Cartwright frowned again.

"No, I can't say—" He caught his breath, and then added roughly: "That's the name of the baby killed last week."

"Yes," Roger said.

"What a swinish thing to suggest," Cartwright growled, and his self-control seemed near breaking point.

"Mr Cartwright, we have a baby-killer to find," Roger said coldly. "And we'll find him."

Cartright said: "I was at home all the evening of last Friday. It was very wet, and there was a good television programme on."

"I see," Roger said non-committally. "Thank you."

Cartwright went out, obviously very uneasy, and Ledbetter said: "He's not too happy, anyhow."

"We'll have his flat watched before he gets there," Roger said, and glanced at the gold wristwatch which reflected the electric light just above his head. "Half-past ten – hm. Shouldn't think there's a lot we can find out about Cartwright tonight, but we'll have to be after his employers, relations and friends tomorrow." Unexpectedly, he stifled a yawn. "Looks as if I'm tired," he remarked as if with surprise. "Gibson, you stay here until relief comes from the Yard. I'll fix it all on the radio."

"Thanks," said Gibson.

"We'll hold Cartwright until your chaps come," promised Ledbetter. "Thanks, Handsome. Want to know something?"

"You think we've got our man."

"I do. No sign of forced entry at doors or windows, so the killer had a key. I've checked that the street door was always kept locked, and so was the front door of the flat. It really means that someone had two keys. And he's got no alibi for last week. I wouldn't be surprised if he did that, too. It's in the bag, Handsome. You can have a good night's sleep."

"Thanks," Roger said dryly.

He went out the back way. Only the police were on duty there. Most of the lights had been put out, and there was much more darkness, while a wind had sprung up, and was blustering through some bushes in a garden next door. Roger, still brisk, walked alone back to his car. He liked spells when he was on his own, and when he could let his thoughts run freely. Ideas came to him more often in moments like these than when he was talking or arguing. He was by nature an individualist, and that had sometimes nearly wrecked his career at the Yard; in other ways, it had made it. For years he had been the youngest Chief Inspector, now he was the youngest Superintendent. There were those who called him a white-haired boy and a Home Office favourite; in fact they knew and he knew that he often acquired a kind of sixth sense about a case. Like this one, for instance.

Everything had fitted neatly in place; click, click, click. The way the mother had looked at Cartwright, the way Cartwright had appeared to be putting on an act, the fact that he had been at the flat earlier and had quarrelled, the fact that he admitted thinking that the baby had come between him and his love. Motive, opportunity, passion: what a case for a jury of women!

Roger reached his car, and as he did so a shadowy figure appeared from the porch of a house a few yards along. He was not easily scared, but the suddenness of the movement and the way the man came swinging towards him did cause a flash of alarm.

Then Roger relaxed, grinning at his own jumpiness.

This was Spendlove, of the *Globe*, probably here to woo an exclusive sentence or two. He stood out as the most competent, as well as the most likable, of the regular crime reporters on Fleet Street.

"Hallo, Handsome," he said amiably. "I knew you hadn't arrived by the front door, so you had to be round here. Thanks for the story."

"You have to have one, so you might as well have the right one," Roger said. He took out a packet of cigarettes and proffered it.

"Thanks," said Spendlove. They lit up, and Roger waited for the next question, which was bound to come; the reporter was probably deliberating on exactly how far he could go. The lighted cigarettes glowed very red for a moment, and then Spendlove said: "I've got something for you, in return."

He probably meant it, and Roger's interest quickened, but all he said was: "Thanks."

"Don't mention it," said Spendlove. "You'd find it out sooner or later." He grinned, but Roger felt sure that what he had to say wouldn't be funny. "Cartwright and the man Shaw, father of the other murdered child, were in the same regiment together during national service," he announced. "Odd, isn't it?"

Chapter Four

Coincidence?

Roger could picture young Cartwright's face as the man had realised the significance of the question about last Friday. Had that been cleverly simulated? Had he been acting when he had looked at Anne Kindle? He recalled the great intensity and the strange expression in the brown eyes. He could picture the horror in the woman's eyes, as if she knew, rather than suspected, that Cartwright had killed her child.

Was that right? Or was he jumping to conclusions? If she had known, even if she had reasonable suspicion, would she have tried to conceal his name, and help him?

"Not surprised?" asked Spendlove.

"Very interested," Roger admitted. "Where did you get the information?"

"Cartwright."

"Eh?"

Spendlove grinned in the poor light.

"You won't have to jump down Ledbetter's throat for missing anything obvious, Handsome. I got it from Cartwright because I know him. I know Shaw, too. We're all in the Territorials, and I act as the local P.R.O. I can't go through all the square bashing and the training, my job being what it is, but I like to lend a hand, and I get down to the drill hall every other week. That's why I covered the Shaw case last week, and why I covered this. I'm a local boy."

"Were they friends?" asked Roger.

"Not particularly."

"Cartwright got any reason to dislike Shaw?"

"Not that I know of," Spendlove answered.

Roger said: "I don't know how useful it will come in, but thanks. And keep it to yourself for the time being, will you? That must make Cartwright older than he looks," he went on.

"He's twenty-four."

"Could be taken for twenty-one," Roger remarked. "How much more do you know about him?"

Spendlove took his cigarette from his lips, hesitated, put it back and drew so that the light showed brightly, and then tossed it into the roadway, where it made a miniature pyrotechnic display.

"Don't misunderstand me," he said carefully. "I know all about the path of duty and assisting the police in the course of their work, but I can save you a lot of checking and double checking, and I know how you like to get a move on. If I tell all, do I get special consideration with news?"

Roger took a long time to answer, and then said: "No."

"You're putting an awful strain on my conscience."

"I'll trust your conscience, and you trust mine," Roger said.

Spendlove grinned more broadly, knowingly, and began briskly: "No barter, but if I happen to be in the right place at the right time, it won't do me any harm. All right, Handsome. Roy Cartwright is a kind of apprentice in a family business. He's an orphan, and has been for years, but his uncle on his mother's side runs a business called Maddison Brothers. They're carpet importers and exporters. It's a big business, most reputable, and quite a dollar earner. Roy has been through most of the departments, and spent twelve months in the midlands, Kidderminster I think, studying carpet making at the factory. He's been through the sales side, and now he's going through the administrative side. Likely to be there for another year or two, as far as I can tell you. He's worked from the London office in Mill Street, near the Bank, for many years. That's how he got to know Anne Kindle. In his way, Cartwright's quite a plum. Must be worth a few thousand in his own right, and he has a substantial share in the business. Yet Anne, as you were about to observe, turned him down and remained faithful to a chirpy merchant sailor who is seldom home."

"Know anything about Cartwright as a person?"

"Not much. Nothing against him. He's an amateur actor and once had ambitions for the stage, but I gather that the uncle discouraged him and he didn't force the issue. Honest enough, but why shouldn't he be? No side, but a bit conscious of the fact that he's a cut above the average socially. A little bit of a snob in all but his love."

Spendlove's pause was obviously to make Roger prompt him. Roger kept silent.

"Have it your own way," went on Spendlove good-humouredly. "He's hot stuff at commando tactics, and that lean body of his is like steel."

"Sure?"

"Positive."

"Thanks," Roger said, and tossed his cigarette away and trod on it before the sparks really flew. "The thing I'm most interested in is whether he ever had any reason to dislike Shaw, and whether he knows Mrs Shaw and ever thought he was in love with her."

"Shouldn't think so," said Spendlove, "but I'll see what I can find out."

"Thanks," said Roger again, and asked: "Give you a lift anywhere?"

"Thanks, but my chariot's round the corner. How are those boys of yours?"

Warmth leapt into Roger's voice.

"Couldn't be better. One of them passed his General Certificate the other day, although we never thought he'd make it."

"That sounds like young Richard," Spendlove remarked.

"You know them as well as that," marvelled Roger. "Your daughter walking again yet?"

"Just beginning to. That kid has all the guts it takes," answered Spendlove. "Well, okay, Handsome. Be seeing you."

The newspaper man turned and walked off, taking very long strides, as if he did not want to continue to talk about his daughter, who had been stricken with poliomyelitis a few months earlier. That was something that he, Roger, Spendlove, Gibson, the man Shaw and Mrs Kindle had in common: children, love of them and fear for them. Roger got into his car, feeling oddly uneasy, as if there was some kind of threat to his own boys which he could not anticipate. It was a form of nervous reaction, of course; he would not forget Mrs Kindle's screams, or her attempt to throw herself out of the window, but he could not afford to dwell on that. He started the engine of his Humber Hawk, a fairly new car, and let in the clutch. There was no need to go back to the Yard. All he need do was check if anything big had come in, and if it hadn't, go home and ponder all he had discovered, and all that Spendlove had told him. The fact that there was a kind of line which connected the two baby murders and Cartwright was the heaven-sent suspect who would make Ledbetter clap his hands with hearty satisfaction, making him feel certain that his early hunch was right.

Roger flicked on the radio, heard a babble of voices, called the Yard and was answered immediately.

"West here." He gave orders for Cartwright's flat to be watched, and for Gibson to be relieved, feeling quite sure that unless Cartwright realised that he was being followed, and set out deliberately to shake his tailer off, all his movements would be reported. The best tailer in the world couldn't hold the trail of a man who meant to elude him. "Is there anything in for me?"

"Nothing at all, sir."

"Then I'm going home. Good-night."

"Good-night, sir," the operator said.

It was a clear night, and there was little traffic about. He put his foot down, and touched fifty; any ordinary citizen caught doing that would get a ten-pound fine. The reflection slowed him down. The truth was that he needed something to quieten fears which really amounted to a presentiment. He had known the mood often enough before and it had seldom been justified, but he would not be really easy in his mind until he reached his own home and made sure that everything was all right. He left the radio on, and the babble ebbed and flowed, but there was no call for him.

Why should there be?

Two babes in arms had been murdered, and the fact had got under his skin. This kind of crime always did. He knew exactly what Gibson meant, and shared his feelings: sane or mad, such a killer did not deserve to live; but society would protect him. There were times when it appeared to be a lunatic world.

And there were times, like this, when he wondered if the killer would strike again; deep down, that was his basic fear. He would be relieved and almost exhilarated if Roy Cartwright was proved to be the murderer, and the case could be filed.

He turned into Bell Street, Chelsea a little after twelve o'clock, caught himself out in a yawn, saw only one light on anywhere in sight, and remembered that it was the bedroom of a young married couple who were having bad nights with their firstborn. Last night that would have made him smile. He swung his wheel out, to turn into the gateway and his own small garage, glancing at the front door of his detached house as the headlights shone on it. There was only darkness; everything was all right, of course. He felt a momentary lift of spirit, and then the babble on his radio was interrupted, and a man said clearly: "Calling Superintendent West. Will Superintendent West come in, please."

Roger flicked his transmitter switch.

"West speaking." This way, he had at least avoided telephone calls at the house, and waking Janet; nothing short of an explosion would wake the boys. Against that, there was the time, the fact that he had been on the go since half-past eight this morning, and the fact that he really needed a few hours of quiet thought, to decide on the best way to handle this case.

"Chief Inspector Gibson would like a word with you, sir; hold on please."

"Right." They would be getting Gibson on the telephone, and connecting him with the walkie-talkie; the ways of crime detection got better and better. Gibson wouldn't call for the sake of it, either.

"Mr West?" His voice was hardly distorted at all.

"Speaking."

"Cartwright's on the run, sir."

"Sure?"

"No doubt about it, sir. He was in a sports car, a new MG, and when he realised that he was being followed, he hared off."

"Damned fool," said Roger, although this was what he had anticipated. "Got a call out?"

"All ready when you say the word," said Gibson.

"I'm saying the word," Roger told him. "When he's picked up, take him along to Cannon Row, let him cool his heels for three or four hours, and then telephone me. I'll come right over."

"Yes, sir," Gibson said.

Roger flicked the radio off, started the engine again, and turned into his drive. This made it look certain that Roy Cartwright was the man they wanted, and it ought to make him feel good, but in fact it didn't. He left the car outside the garage, so that he could get out again in a hurry when he was called, and then opened the front door of the house very stealthily. A strong smell of new paint greeted him. He always managed to forget that they were having the decorators in; Janet was blueing his first year's extra salary as a Superintendent. He went along to the kitchen, found coffee all ready to heat, sandwiches under a silver-plated dish cover, and a bottle of whisky and a syphon of soda on the kitchen table. The whisky would make him sleep, the coffee would keep him awake, just as it would keep Janet awake if she drank it too near bedtime. He needed the two hours or so of sleep that he would get.

When he crept into his bedroom, anxious not to disturb Janet, he remembered the way he had gone on tiptoe, sixteen years or so ago, when Janet had been nursing the boys and sleep had been vital to her. He closed the door silently, listened to her steady breathing, and then felt a sudden onrush of mingled dread and self-blame.

What the hell was the matter with him?

Cartwright had gone on the run, and all the police in London would be on the look-out for him now, but he hadn't given a serious thought to the real danger: that if he were the killer, he might strike again tonight. It wasn't a question of bringing him in, and letting him cool his heels; his capture was desperately urgent.

Nothing he could do would help, though; it would be a waste of time going back to the Yard. He probably wouldn't be able to sleep, but he would get over that, and might even get some ideas. In fact, he was drowsy as soon as he got into bed next to Janet. Her body warmth seemed to steal over him, and make him forget the pressing anxieties and the fears.

Cartwright would soon be caught, he told himself; in a couple of hours the telephone bell would ring. He went to sleep.

A few miles away, in one of London's more beautiful dormitory towns, a young mother lay awake, hearing her husband snore faintly, and looking at the open door of the bedroom. There was no whimper of sound, nothing to tell her of the baby, sleeping in its cot. After a while, she got out of bed and crept to the door, across the passage where there was a dim light, and into the nursery.

Her baby was there.

She stood peering down, and absolutely still – until the telephone bell jolted her into movement. Desperately anxious not to have the child disturbed, she dashed out and into her husband's study, snatched up the telephone, and gasped: "Who is it? Who—"

"Look after your baby," a man said. "It might be next on the list."

When her husband came hurrying, she looked shocked and frightened.

Chapter Five

Headlines

It was broad daylight when Roger woke, and at first he could not understand why he was startled at finding that, and why it seemed wrong. Janet was sleeping with her back to him, so it wasn't yet seven o'clock; on weekdays her mind was like an alarm clock, for seven. He heard the chink of milk bottles in the street, and then realised what was on his mind.

He hadn't been called: so Roy Cartwright hadn't been caught. No one at the Yard was so soft-hearted that they would 'forget' to call him.

Roger went downstairs for his inevitable morning chore if he were up first: to make the tea. He looked for the papers at the front door, but they had not arrived. He hurried upstairs again, and glanced in at the boy's room. Martin, called Scoopy, his elder boy, now over fifteen, looked as if he were outgrowing his bed; one bare foot was stuck out of the clothes at one side, and his big arms were raised above his head, the backs of his fingers touching the wall. He was fast asleep. Richard, called Richard, just a year younger, was snuggled so deeply beneath his clothes that only the top of his dark head showed. Roger pushed the sheets back from his face, and the boy stirred but did not wake. He was breathing through his slightly open mouth; catarrh or hay fever, or whatever they called it, was a constant trouble to him.

Roger went out.

He could not get his mind off the fact that Cartwright was missing. He could imagine what Ledbetter was feeling: 'I told you so'. Ledbetter had felt sure from the start that Cartwright was the man they wanted. If he were, and if another child died, then part of the responsibility would be his, Roger's.

He heard footsteps outside, and went downstairs to see the newspapers, the *Globe* and the *Gazette,* poking through the letter box. The whistling kettle was beginning to squeal. He had to open the door to get the newspapers out, and one of them caught. He tugged, and tore it. In a bad mood, he hurried along the passage because the kettle was now whistling shrilly, and he knew from experience that the sound was likely to wake Janet. He snatched off the whistling cap, and the steam stung his fingers.

He swore as he shook them.

Something about his attitude and his mood suddenly made him grin.

"You go on like this and you'll give them a hell of a day at the office," he said to himself, and let the kettle boil silently while he opened the *Globe*. The baby murder was a front-page story, of course, skilfully written and presented; Spendlove had kept his part of the bargain. Martha Wise's *Gazette* was less predictable. Roger opened it, and the headline which seemed to leap out at him was exactly the one he had hoped to avoid.

BABY-KILLER AT LARGE

Were they taking a chance of libel against Cartwright?

He read the story, written by chunky grey-haired Aunt Martha. It was sob-stuff, but it was good. Every young mother who read this would have a surge of anxiety, perhaps of fear. Every cot and pram would be guarded with especial care today. Well, why not? But supposing this was the angle the *Gazette* intended to take all the way through? It was after new readers, it lived on sensation, and there wasn't a trick unknown to it or its staff. Roger skimmed through the story, but found no mention of Cartwright, only of 'a man' being questioned by the police. There was a photograph of Anne Kindle and the child in her arms, a big picture probably enlarged from a snapshot, for the edges were so badly blurred; but it was impossible to mistake the identity of the woman. He made the tea.

Janet was snuggling down in bed, but awake. "Ugh," she grunted.

"Hallo," Roger said, and bent over and kissed her forehead lightly. "You're as bad as Scoop." He put the tray down on a bedside table, and tossed the newspapers on to the bed. "Been awake long?"

"I woke when you got up," Janet asserted, and now she sounded more wide awake. "What's up?"

"Nothing."

"Don't be silly," Janet said, and sat upright. Her dark hair was showing quite a lot of grey, but was still very plentiful, and its natural wave was her chief pride. Her hair net, of pale pink, was pushed a little to one side. She looked sleepy, although her eyes were alert. She was attractive and finely built, and she clutched a woollen bedjacket from the chair by her side, draped it round her shoulders, and went on: "What time did you get in?"

"Twelve-ish," Roger said.

"Did you have a nasty case?"

Roger showed her the *Gazette* front page, could guess the immediate reaction; she actually winced. Their youngest child was nearly fifteen, but it could catch her as sharply as that. She scanned the story, then looked up at him.

"Have you caught the man?"

"I may have let him get away."

"Oh," said Janet, and he knew that she understood the fear that was passing through his mind. He could say to her what he could not possibly say at the Yard; she was a kind of safety valve. "I could see there was something," she went on, and glanced back at the paper. "The mother looks very young."

"Twenty-four," Roger told her quietly. "Sweet, I'm going to have a quick shave, and then get off to the Yard in a hurry. Mind getting my breakfast before you dress? I'll tell you what it's all about as I have it."

"Of course," Janet said.

Three-quarters of an hour later, as a clock was striking eight, Roger went out to the garage. He felt less tense, because he had talked freely. Janet had gone upstairs to change and to get the boys up; they were likely to be late this morning, but that was no change. As he opened the doors of the car, parked where he had left it for the expected night trip, he heard a window bang up and his younger son call: "Good-bye, Dad!"

"'Bye, old chap! See you tonight."

"Hope so!"

Then Martin's hands appeared on the younger boy's shoulder. Richard was moved aside as if he were a feather, while Martin filled the whole window, his fair hair sticking up in its morning dishevelment, grinning at some protest from his brother. He waved and called: "Any chance of being home for supper?"

"I'll try to."

Richard's head appeared, over Martin's shoulder; he was grinning, too. They were a good-natured, good-tempered, happy pair. Roger started the engine, reversed, and headed for the Yard. Very little traffic was about, there were more cyclists than motor-cars, and only one or two buses. He kept to the main roads, not the Thames Embankment, which he would have used during a busier period. The boys and Janet had taken his mind off the immediate anxiety, but it was still there, and it went deep. He could not shrug off the fact that there had been good grounds for detaining Cartwright, and for taking him to the Yard for questioning, but that he had lost the chance.

The day shift men had just come on duty at the Yard, and there was briskness in the way they greeted him, in their movements. He had used the Embankment entrance, parked close to the foot of the steps, and hurried up into the big 'new' building. Sergeants on duty in the hall looked as if they were very glad to see him. He met no senior officers, and when he went into his own office, it was empty and very tidy. Gibson, who shared it with him as his second-in-command, had probably been out most of the night. Roger saw the newspapers spread out on his desk, and looked through the headlines, to find that one other paper had taken the same angle as the *Gazette*; the others had followed Spendlove. He called Information.

"Anything fresh in about Cartwright?"

"No, sir."

"Damn it, he can't have vanished into thin air."

"No, sir," the man repeated; there wasn't much else he could say.

"Any word of his car?"

"No, sir."

Roger said: "Well, put this out as a general message: find where Cartwright usually garaged his car, and find out what other garages he would usually have had access to. Make sure that all builders' yards, garages and possible parking places are covered. Get all Divisions on to that, quick."

"Yes, sir."

Roger grunted: "Thanks," and rang off. The truth was that nothing would put him in a good humour until he had found Cartwright. And he would want to concentrate on the job. He pushed the newspapers aside, and opened the first of the folders on his desk; Gibson shared his obsession for tidiness and it helped to get the work done more quickly. These were reports on the various jobs going through, and unless something exceptional had happened during the night, half an hour would be time enough to deal with them. After that he could have a word with the Commander of the Criminal Investigation Department, Hardy, and put everything aside except the Cartwright job.

Then, he saw a memo, from Gibson, which read:

8.10. Message received from Ledbetter about a missing baby. Have gone to AS Division to check. Have asked murder team to stand by on your instructions.

Roger's heart contracted; this might be the dreaded development, although this baby was missing, not dead. Would the killer of the Shaw and Kindle babies take a victim away?

He stared at the message and read it until he had it off by heart. It was twenty to nine. Gibson, sound and unflurried, had not harassed him on the road, but handled the situation this way, after trying to get him by telephone. A radio call to him while on the road would have been picked up by all the Divisions, and it would have been known at once that Roger West had dropped a clanger; there were plenty who would find cause for satisfaction in that.

He picked up one of the three telephones on his desk.

"Get me Mr Ledbetter, of AS."

"I'll call you, sir."

Roger put down the receiver, and began to look through the reports on the other cases; the clearing up of a robbery in Kent, some reports on a poison pen investigation, notes from the City Police about a suspected share fraud, and Divisional reports on a variety of cases. The telephone bell did not ring. No one came in to see him, but it was early yet. There was a report signed *P.C. Loratt, Police Officer, AS Division B Station,* which gave a few details about Mrs Kindle's neighbours, husband and friends: this was from the constable he had spoken to last night. He scribbled a note asking Ledbetter to give the man a pat on the back, then looked impatiently at the telephone. Ledbetter was probably out on the job, and almost certainly irritable because he had been called out early after a late night. The pressures at the Divisions were as great as those at the Yard.

The telephone bell rang and Roger took up the receiver quickly.

"West here."

"I can't get Mr Ledbetter, sir, he's out on a case, but Mr Gibson is asking for you."

"Put him through."

"Yes, sir."

Gibson was as dependable as he was solid physically; a man who grew on one. Roger had not particularly liked him when they had first met, had not been sure that they would make a good team; he had no doubts now.

"Hallo, Gibby."

"I've had a look at the new baby case," Gibson said, "and I don't think it's connected with the Kindle job." Roger wondered if the other man had even the slightest idea what a relief that was. "The baby's older, nearly a year. There's no sign of the body, and it looks like an abduction. I've got a suspicion that the father knows all about it – it's one of the broken home jobs. But if you don't mind me saying so, I think you ought to come over. Ledbetter's on the scene himself, and it would calm him down a bit."

Roger found himself grinning.

"I'll come. Where are you?"

'Tenfold Street, Ealing Common."

"Give me half an hour," said Roger.

He had swung from depression to a kind of gaiety in two minutes, and it made no difference that, in its way, this was as great a tragedy as last night's. The important thing was that he need not feel responsible for what had happened to this child.

But there might be others. This made no difference to the great urgency of the need for finding Roy Cartwright. He wasn't even sure that he should go to see Ledbetter; it might be wiser to concentrate on Cartwright. He put in a call to the nursing home where Anne Kindle had been taken, was told that she was still sleeping, made one or two notes for the Commander, and went out. It would probably be wise to make Ledbetter sweet. It was a clear, bright, late spring morning, a good-to-be-alive morning, and he ran down the steps of the C.I.D. building with as much ease and lightheartedness as Scoop or Richard would have done. He was actually at the door of the car when he heard his name called from the top of the steps. Perhaps Cartwright had been found.

He turned, and shouted: "Hallo?"

"Message for you, sir." A bare-headed, fair-haired uniformed sergeant came hurrying, a big man who looked ungainly, being slightly knock-kneed. Roger went to meet him, and the man was a little breathless as he went on: "The MG sports car belonging to Roy Cartwright has been found."

Roger said: "Oh. Where?"

"In the Thames up by Duke's Meadows, Chiswick, sir. Looks as if it was driven straight in."

"Cartwright?"

"No message about him," the sergeant answered.

Chapter Six

Case to Case

"Ask the Chiswick chaps not to move anything until I've had a look myself," Roger said to the sergeant. "Say I expect to be over in about an hour." It might prove to be an hour and a half, but that would seem too long a time for the Divisional people to wait, and he might be able to get the job at Penfold Street finished quicker than he expected.

The traffic was much thicker coming into London, and he was held up at every traffic light on the way to Shepherd's Bush, but from there to Ealing Common the road was much clearer. At twenty minutes to ten, Roger was in Penfold Street. Several cars were pulled up halfway along a street of Victorian terrace houses, all larger and more pretentious than those where Anne Kindle lived. There was a small crowd of people; and he wasn't surprised to see Aunt Martha and Spendlove.

Aunt Martha gave her most gentle, beguiling smile.

"Good-morning, Superintendent."

"Why don't you go and write a nice article advising all the mothers of babes in arms to put their heads in gas ovens?" Roger asked.

"I'd rather write one telling them that you've caught Cartwright," retorted Aunt Martha.

Roger grinned. "Well, don't blame me if you're wasting your time." He winked at Spendlove so that the *Globe* man alone could see it, and felt sure that Spendlove would realise that it had more significance than just a wink. "Nice story you did," he said, to the man. "Perhaps your editor's less of a sadist." He nodded to a uniformed constable standing in the doorway of the house, and went in. This was large, airy, and well-furnished.

"Where's Mr Ledbetter?"

"First floor, sir," the constable told him.

Roger hurried upstairs, listening intently, hearing a murmur of voices, and then a sharp exclamation in a woman's voice. Several doors led from the large landing and one was ajar. Inside were Ledbetter, Gibson, a plain-clothes officer and a woman of about the same age as Anne Kindle; perhaps a year or so older.

Perhaps twenty years older, for she looked as if she had aged overnight. There was a haggard expression in her eyes, her mouth was taut, her bottom lip kept quivering. She was standing in a wide bay window, hands moving, legs twitching, glancing right and left. Here was tragedy, stark and inescapable.

The woman saw him come in, and exclaimed as if newly frightened: "Who's this?"

"Superintendent West of Scotland Yard, Mrs Lee," Ledbetter said. He looked fresh and perky; perhaps he'd had a good night's sleep too. He nodded to Roger and went on: "Mrs Lee is afraid that her husband is responsible for—"

"I know it's him – who else would do a thing like this?" demanded the woman shrilly. "What's the use of standing there and saying you think this or you think that? Why don't you try to find my baby? Why haven't you been to my husband's flat? Why—"

"We have, Mrs Lee," Ledbetter managed to say.

"Then where's my baby? Where—" The woman broke off, as if she knew the answer to that only too well but did not want to have to admit it. Her eyes were red-rimmed and sore-looking, and she seemed unbearably nervous and edgy; she simply couldn't keep still. "You've got to find Thomas. You've *got* to. My husband said he'd rather see him dead than with me, and he meant it; if you knew my husband you'd know that he meant it. He wasn't sane, that's why I had to leave him. He simply wasn't sane, and there's no telling what he'll do." She caught her breath. *"Why don't you go and find my baby?"*

Roger asked: "What's been fixed, Superintendent?"

"Nothing yet. We're trying to find out if anyone saw who broke into the house during the night, or if anyone heard or saw a car," Ledbetter answered. "Mrs Lee put the baby to bed at half-past ten last night, after its late feed, and there was no sign of it this morning at eight o'clock."

"I thought Thomas was sleeping on," Mrs Lee interrupted shrilly. "Usually he wakes me at six o'clock and I'm tired to death. I was only too glad of an extra hour. I couldn't believe he'd slept so late, but I didn't go right into him; if he was still asleep it seemed a pity to disturb him. And then when I went to the room he wasn't there!"

She began to beat her hands against her forehead.

Roger said to Gibson: "Go and talk to the Yard, and have a general call put out for the husband – ports, airfields, stations, everything." Gibson nodded and went off, and Roger waited for the woman to stop beating herself; he doubted whether she had heard what he had said. Did all women react like this? He knew they didn't; he remembered a time when there had been fear that one of his own boys had been taken away and killed. Janet had gone silent, and in a way that had been worse than this kind of outburst.

"I've been telling Mrs Lee that we'll do everything we can," Ledbetter said, "and that she needn't worry."

"But he said he'd rather see Thomas dead!" screeched Mrs Lee.

"You'll find that he didn't mean it," Ledbetter tried to persuade her. "Now, if you'll tell us where we're likely to find your husband, if he's not at home—"

"I don't know! All I want is my baby back!"

She wouldn't be much good until she had been given a sedative, and she would certainly fight against taking one. It would probably be better for a policewoman to talk to her, and try to ease her out of this hysteria. The policewoman came in, and then there was a flurry of sound downstairs, a woman's voice, and then a cry from Mrs Lee, who flung herself towards the door and went running down the stairs.

Ledbetter grimaced.

"That's her mother," he declared. "This is her parents' place. The father's in a nursing home, the mother's been staying near him. Hell of a job, but this really does look cut and dried. I needn't have brought you over."

Roger said: "Glad you did. Anything at all to make it look like Cartwright now?"

"Not a thing. When I was woken up at home and told a baby was missing, I blew my top," Ledbetter said. "But soon after I got here, I realised that this wasn't the same kind of job. What gets into a man to steal his own wife's baby from her like this?"

Roger said: "We'd all like to know. Nothing to do but look for Lee, is there?"

"No."

"Did you know that Cartwright's car had been found in the Thames at Chiswick?"

"Good God!" exclaimed Ledbetter. "Has he killed himself?"

"Could be," agreed Roger, and drove off, glad that the Lee case had not taken more time.

The car had been pulled out of the river by ropes and a winch. The Land Rover, on which the winch was placed, was still at hand, with a shirt-sleeved driver smoking a cigarette which drooped from the corner of his mouth. He looked rather like a gypsy, with a dark skin, very curly hair and bright, dark brown eyes. A dozen police had gathered, and there was the inevitable crowd of onlookers, who had heard what had happened and found their way across the fields. The Thames was wide just here. Almost opposite was the Mortlake Brewery, and in front of that was the tow-path, deserted and not even remindful of the teeming crowds which gathered there on Boat Race Day. The river was sparkling in the sunlight, the young leaves of the nearby trees seemed fresh and friendly, the whole place had an atmosphere of summer picnics and a promise of night's passion.

The Chiswick Divisional police were spread over the meadows, obviously tracing the way the car had come. A chief inspector,

Greenways, was an elderly man whom Roger knew well; grey-haired, sleek, almost smooth. He shook hands.

"Just inside the hour," he said. "Thanks."

"Glad I could make it. Found anything?"

"Only what you can see. If it had been a saloon car we'd have found the body in it, but this way – well, he might have pushed it over, although we don't think it was pushed; it looked as if it was driven until the last moment. The gear was in neutral. If he were in it, he could have been washed away, or he could have swum to safety. Damned unsatisfactory."

"What makes you say it looks as if it was driven?"

"Come and see," Greenways invited.

Heavy rain two days ago had made the bank of the river muddy, and there were bare patches on the grass near the water. The tracks of the tyres of the MG were clear; so were tracks, ten yards away, where it had been dragged out of the river. The first track looked fairly even. Roger knew that if a man, or even two or three men, had pushed it, while one had guided the wheel, there would have been spots where the wheels caught against lumps of grass, and skidded slightly, or else slid over the patch just in front or behind the lump. The front tracks would have been a little irregular, too; it was impossible to guide a car absolutely straight while walking alongside it. Two minutes was enough to let Roger say: "Not much doubt about it, it was driven in."

"Can't imagine him driving it in and then trying to get out, can you?" asked Greenaways. "I'd say he was in a pretty hysterical frame of mind. Not much doubt he killed that baby, realised what he'd done, and did himself in."

Greenways would not say this to a junior, or to the Press, but obviously he believed it, and to argue would be to invite scepticism, and perhaps a kind of resentment. Roger said: "Could be, but I'd like to find the body. Started dragging any likely places?"

"I've laid it on," answered Greenways, "but you'd better get the River boys busy on this; the body probably floated downstream. It was about ebb tide at midnight, so it could be anywhere between here and Greenwich. Running pretty fast, too; we were flooded here last week."

"Can see you were," said Roger.

Questions were building themselves up in his mind. If Cartwright wanted to make it look as if he were dead, this was exactly how he would try. If he were as good an actor as Ledbetter thought, then he might have done it. But what would follow? Unless the murder of the baby had been carefully premeditated, he couldn't have made plans to escape; and he had a lot to leave behind. A useful sum in capital and another in a share of the family business.

"No sign of anyone else's prints," Greenways said. "I've been over it. Most of the prints were gone, but a few on the steering wheel and the gear lever hand showed up plainly enough. Nothing at all to suggest that anyone but Cartwright drove this here – we got his dabs from Mrs Kindle's place." The Divisional man's manner suggested that he thought Roger was in some doubt.

"Looks cut and dried," Roger conceded. "Have you found anything in the car?"

"Haven't looked – we do what you Yard VIP's tell us."

Roger grinned.

"When it suits you!" He moved to the car, and with Greenways looked in the dashboard pocket, the door pockets, and the boot; anywhere they might find articles of interest. There were the usual odds and ends: an A.A. book, a map-reader, matches, keys, cigarettes, dusters, a small screwdriver, two half-finished packets of fruit lozenges; no names, nothing to help the police at all.

"Tell you what," said Roger. "I'm going to leave all the rest to you." He grinned again. "Let me have a copy of all reports at the Yard, won't you?"

"Glad to do your work for you, Handsome!" Greenways turned, and then frowned. "Oh, Gawd, look who's here. Does it matter if he gets the story?"

Spendlove was wobbling towards them on a bicycle; so he had obviously checked where he was likely to find Roger. He looked big and ungainly on the bicycle, and unexpectedly it occurred to Roger that he was an ugly man, although he had never thought that before.

He had a big nose, once broken and pushed a little to one side. He was smiling when he pulled up.

"Did anyone tell you that Greenways hates me?"

"Who's surprised?" asked Roger.

"That's what I like to hear," said Greenways.

"Soulless types, you coppers," Spendlove said. "So you've found Cartwright's car but not Cartwright himself. Mind if I take a few details?"

"I'm on my way," Roger said. "If it's all right with Superintendent Greenways, it's all right with me." He shook hands with Greenways, and then strode across the meadows towards his car, which was parked with several other police cars in a side road leading from Chiswick High Street.

It had been urgent enough to find Cartwright before; it was vital now.

The most likely people to know where he might be, if he were still alive, were the members of the firm of Maddison Brothers. Ah! They were importers and exporters of carpets, remember, and would have a great deal of work at the London Docks. Cartwright was likely to be able to find his way about the docks, then.

Roger got into his car, watched by two boys of about thirteen, who looked as if they should be at school. They irritated him, but before driving off he flicked on the radio and called the Yard. The two boys edged nearer, obviously to try to hear what he said: he kept his voice low.

"West here ... I'm on my way to Maddison Brothers, the carpet firm ... Ask the River Division to keep a sharp look-out for the body of Roy Cartwright, or any of his clothes," Roger said. "You've got the description."

The boys were pressing very close; if the Yard asked him to repeat that, they would be bound to hear. He waved them away, but they ignored him. He saw how their eyes glistened, sensed their excitement.

"Message understood, sir."

"Thanks," said Roger, and switched off. "Now, you two—"

The smaller of the pair asked, explosively: "You *are* Superintendent West of the Yard, aren't you?"

"Yes, but—"

"*Could* we have your autograph, sir, please?"

Roger was startled into a laugh, signed a small autograph album and a scrap of paper, and drove off. Then he sobered. This pair had been babes in arms once; mothers had been anxious, frightened, fearful for them. As Janet had, over their boys.

He was wondering what Cartwright's uncle would be like when a flash came for him over the radio. He answered, hoping that this was news of Cartwright.

It was the Yard's Information Office.

"Special message for you, sir," the caller announced. "A Mrs Edward Maddison reported a threat to her infant son last night. She is the wife of Mr Edward Maddison, of Esher, Surrey, and the senior member of the firm of Maddison Brothers. I understand you are on your way to see Maddisons now, and thought you should know this at once."

"You couldn't have been more right," Roger said fervently.

That gave him more than he wanted to think about.

It was nearly half-past twelve when he found a parking place near the premises of Maddison Brothers. Offices, showrooms and storerooms were in the same building, and some beautiful carpets were draped in the window; one was marked at over six hundred pounds, almost enough money to furnish a whole house. Roger stepped inside, and a frail, silvery-haired man, the type who might well have spent a lifetime in the service of the firm, asked him courteously: "You're not a newspaper reporter, sir, are you? Mr Edward has refused to see any more gentlemen of the Press."

"I'm from Scotland Yard," Roger said. The old man took his card, and asked him to wait in the small office with one window overlooking a carpet showroom. Most of those on show were Persian, but Roger saw an archway with the word *Indian* over it, and another marked: *North African*. He pressed close to the window, saw that the archways led to other rooms, each differently marked, and saw half a dozen people were moving about. There was a curiously subdued atmosphere here, almost one of reverence.

Then the door through which the old man had gone was thrust open. A man who would have been noticeable in any circumstances stepped through. He was exceptionally tall, probably six feet six, was somewhere in the early fifties, and was startlingly good-looking. A monocle, affectation on many, seemed right for him. He wore a dark grey suit, white shirt and pearl-grey tie with a single pearl pin in it. He actually looked down at Roger, as he said: "Mr West?"

"Yes. I'm sorry to—"

"There is nothing I can tell you about my nephew, nothing at all," the tall man asserted. "And as I am extremely busy, I must ask you to excuse me."

There was nothing he could tell the police about the threat to his infant son, either, it seemed.

Chapter Seven

Edward Maddison

This was how things often went, Roger knew; blank, blank, blank, and then a break. The only question was whether to try to force the issue now, or whether to let the handsome Maddison believe that he had carried the day, and work on the white-haired man; a simple matter of tactics. The arrogance in Edward Maddison's manner was unmistakable; he was used to being obeyed without delay or question. Already he was preparing to speak again.

Roger said: "May I have two minutes with you in private, please?"

"I have already told you—"

"This is a very important matter, Mr Maddison, and one that you should know about."

The silvery-haired man was by the counter, hands by his side, eyes darting to and fro; there was a kind of slyness about him. Maddison looked as if he would like to push Roger aside, but something in Roger's manner obviously impressed him, for he turned abruptly, and said: "I have no desire to appear discourteous, but I am in the middle of a board meeting, and have some important overseas customers due to lunch with me in half an hour. It is quite preposterous to think that my nephew could be in any way connected with this murder. I hope that there is no doubt in your mind about that."

He turned, thrust open the door, and led the way up a flight of oak steps. The whole place had the appearance of prosperity. They reached a landing, which opened out into more showrooms, beautifully lighted, and with carpets spread out, or draped, almost as if they were precious things.

A sleek, slender American woman with beautiful legs was standing in the middle of one carpet, and her husband was sitting in a chair, ankles crossed, hat on his lap. The woman was saying: "What do you think, dear?"

Edward Maddison pushed open a door marked: *Private*. This led to a passage, and there were several doors on the right. He opened the second, and led the way into a small but beautifully appointed office, with a Persian carpet on the floor which seemed to purr, panelled walls, and small but equally beautiful carpets draped on the walls. The desk seemed to merge with the walnut panelling, and was intricately carved; it reminded Roger of an old Arab door.

Maddison said: "Now, Mr West, what is this private matter?"

Roger answered quite flatly, watching the grey eyes with much more intentness than Maddison probably realised.

"We have reason to believe that your nephew committed suicide last night, sir."

He had the satisfaction of making Maddison move back a pace; of seeing the finely chiselled lips part; and of seeing the gleam in those cold eyes, which might almost be one of satisfaction. If it were, there followed a masterly piece of dissimulation. Maddison's expression changed on the instant into one of dismay and alarm. He raised one hand, as if to fend off evil tidings. If it was an act, it was slightly over-acted; but then the man was slightly larger than life in every way, and probably his everyday behaviour would seem stagey to many people. He kept quite still, staring at Roger as if trying to discredit what he had said, and when he spoke it was in a very slow, low-pitched voice, which declared that he did not intend to be driven into a panic.

"I refuse to believe that is possible."

"His car was found in the River Thames," Roger announced, but he could not be sure whether this man knew what had happened to the car.

"Are you telling me that my nephew's *body* has been found?"

"All the evidence points—" Roger began.

"Mr West, I do not believe that my nephew committed suicide. If there is any reason to believe that harm has befallen him, then it is either an accidental injury or—one caused by a third party. Roy is not the man to commit suicide, not the one to avoid his responsibilities."

"Such as a charge of murder, sir?"

"Had you charged him with murder?"

"He had reason to suspect that we would."

"I see," said Maddison very slowly, and his voice dropped even lower. "In that case it is conceivable that he was driven to desperate straits. And I hope you are aware whose responsibility that would be, Mr West. What efforts are being made to find out whether he is, in fact, dead?"

Roger said: "Every possible effort."

Maddison had made one mistake, and probably realised it; he was too cold, too unemotional. He was behaving as if he did not care at all what happened to his nephew, and was more interested in scoring off the policeman in front of him. It was often the same: few men were as clever as they believed themselves to be.

"I must ask you not to publish this information or do anything which might distress my wife," Maddison said. "If the worst does come to the worst she will have to know, but, until then, may I rely on your discretion?"

"Did you know of your nephew's association with Mrs Kindle, sir?"

"Yes. And strongly disapproved."

"Is there any history of mental illness in your nephew?"

"There is not," answered Maddison, coolly. "Is there any way in which I can help you look for the boy?"

"You can tell me where he would normally go if he wanted to hide," Roger answered. "The names and addresses of relatives, clubs, friends, parts of the country he liked – all that kind of thing."

"It is quite impossible for me to tell you all of that offhand," said Maddison. "I will arrange for a statement to be made available for you in an hour's time. Will that serve your purpose?"

"Very well, sir, thank you," Roger said. "May I ask one more question, please?"

"If you'll hurry."

"Yes, sir. Why didn't you report that your own baby had been threatened?"

Again there was a momentary glint in Maddison's eyes, as if he had been taken by surprise, but that was gone in a flash, and he said: "I understood that was reported by my wife. I hardly needed to repeat it. Didn't my wife tell you?"

"She reported to the local police, sir, yes. I understand she was in some distress."

"We have an excellent resident staff: a man and wife. I cannot be home all the time, and my wife will come to realise how good the servants are. Mr West, give me your considered opinion: if a man intended to harm a child, would he warn the parents?"

"There's no telling, sir," Roger said woodenly. "I would like to know exactly what happened, please."

Maddison told him, and his responses came pat. No, he had not heard the caller. As far as he knew, there had been no earlier threats. He did not attempt to understand it. Yes, it was strange that his nephew should be suspected of a baby murder, and his, Maddison's, child should be threatened. It was possibly an inverted kind of revenge; bereaved parents did become deranged. He, Maddison, had taken all necessary precautions at home; it was for the police to do the rest.

Roger was not satisfied, but did not force the issue. He was nodding to the silver-haired man twenty-five minutes after he had first entered the office quarters. He turned away from the saleroom entrance as the slim American woman and her bulky husband appeared. A turbanned Sikh was at the door, bowing them out; that was the kind of touch which Roger could well appreciate. He went to his car unhurriedly, for he felt sure that he was being watched, drove off and switched on the radio to the Yard immediately.

"West speaking." His voice was hard and clipped and eager. "Is Mr Gibson there? ... Hallo, Jim, glad you're back. I want the servants and neighbours at Edward Maddison's home watched and checked," he said. "Fix it with the Surrey chaps at once, will you? And I think I may have got a line on young Cartwright," he went on. "I want one of our chaps, smaller than average, and a policewoman, to go to Maddison's carpet warehouse. They're to go as customers, man and wife, say, looking for a special carpet – who've we got who knows anything about carpets?"

"Evans did the big carpet warehouse racket way back," Gibson answered. "He might be recognised, but he knows the place."

"Better send him," Roger decided. "We want all entrances to the premises watched – it's just possible that we might flush Cartwright."

"Why not get a warrant?" asked Gibson.

"I'd rather play it this way," Roger said. "If we produce a warrant Maddison and everyone at the warehouse will be warned. If we do it by stealth, we might find more. If this attempt falls down, though, we can get a warrant soon enough."

"O.K.," Gibson said. "Will you be at the warehouse?"

"I'm going to nip home, change my suit, and return by taxi," Roger answered. "I'll be in the place, but Evans and the woman aren't to recognise me. Right?"

For the first time emotion of a kind sounded in Gibson's voice.

"Wouldn't it be better for me to go?"

Roger said: "No, you—" and then he broke off, grimaced, and realised that what had sounded like envy was really Gibson showing rare tact. He ought not to go himself, much as he would like to. That was one of the drawbacks of a superintendency – he would be stepping into danger because he might be recognised. He did not relish the idea, but in fact this was a job for Gibson, not for him; and when he had talked about changing his clothes, Gibson had seen that; there wasn't a quicker mind at the Yard, although he gave the impression of being so slow-speaking and slow-moving.

"All right," Roger said. "You come over. The whole warehouse wants searching. Pose as a potentially big customer, so that they take you around."

"I will," said Gibson.

He had left the office when Roger reached the Yard, obviously determined not to lose a minute. On Roger's desk was another pile of reports, and several memos from Hardy, about the baby murder case. There was also a note that Mrs Kindle had come round, and a pencilled one in Hardy's handwriting saying: "I should talk to her yourself."

"And I'd better," Roger said aloud.

But he wished that he was with Gibson and the others.

He checked that the exits from the warehouse would be watched, gave instructions that any van leaving with a load of carpets should be stopped when out of sight of the warehouse and searched, and then got up to go and visit Mrs Kindle in the nursing home. He did not relish it at all; her grief would be greater and would show itself in the same way as the other mother's at Ealing Common. There was Maddison's wife, too. Would it be wise to see her, soon? He wanted to know her version of the story, and also to hear what Maddison's reaction to the news had been.

Yet Roger was thinking of Gibson, not the mothers or the babies, as he drove away from the Yard.

Chapter Eight

Carpets

Gibson was thinking about Handsome West when he reached the main entrance to Maddison's warehouse. He saw a bearded Sikh, just inside, standing at attention. On one of the great plate-glass windows two words were written in gold leaf: *Oriental Carpets*. He paused for a moment to look at the two displayed in the window, and then moved towards the door. The Sikh opened it before he could touch the handle, and greeted him in a deep voice with only a hint of accent: "Good-morning, sir. What is your pleasure?"

Gibson said: "I'm from Jasons, of Toronto, and I want to look at some carpets." His voice was much more heavily accented than the Sikh's; an unmistakable Canadian voice. He had spent twenty minutes reading up about carpets and five talking to Evans: the name Jasons was a reasonable one, for it was one of the Canadian department stores who were likely to have or want business with the Maddisons.

"If you will come this way, sir, we will help you," the Sikh said. He was massive and magnificent, and dwarfed Evans, who was standing with a policewoman in plainclothes, Margaret Webb, of the C.I.D., and studying carpets which were probably worth more than his year's salary. The Sikh led the way to a small partitioned office, where a bald-headed man sat at a small desk, forehead wrinkled, unbelievably pre-occupied. On the window of the partition was some lettering in gold leaf: *North America*. Similar small offices were partitioned off round the walls of this large room, and each was marked in much the same way; Gibson noted with respect the thoroughness of this organisation.

The bald-headed man's forehead smoothed out instantly when they stopped at his door.

"From Jasons, sir – yes, of course, I know the firm very well. We have a small account with you, and naturally we would do all we could to make it larger! What particular kind of carpet are you interested in?"

"What I would like is a chance to look round and see what you've got and whether you're competitive in price," Gibson announced.

"I'll gladly procure a guide to take you to all departments," the little man promised.

The guide was introduced to Gibson as Miss Osborn. She was a slim, willowy young woman with a mass of gold-coloured hair, a touch of severity, a smooth complexion, beautiful teeth and a look which suggested that all kinds of things happened in the warehouse and she was quite used to keeping men at their distance. She walked a little ahead of Gibson, whose eyes dropped to her legs; they were quite beautiful. She had a little wobble, partly because of spike-heeled shoes; probably she asked for whatever she got.

"Just a quick look first will suit me very well," Gibson said, "and we can go back to anything that interests me."

"Very good, sir." The guide was very prim.

Gibson could imagine how much West wished that he were here. West was a terror for wanting to be in the thick of a job like this; superintendency kept him tied to his desk too often. Gibson, keeping the girl in sight appreciatively, looked round while he examined the carpets and the girl gave the obvious sales talk about quality, beauty, price. He saw pile upon pile of great carpets, and was astonished at the size of the warehouse; it was like a great honeycomb of different salons. Evans had given him some idea what to expect; carpets from a dozen different places in India, from Pakistan, Turkey, Persia, all parts of the Middle East, from China, Yugoslavia, from South America. Going round, Gibson began to realise the extent of the business which Maddison Brothers did. In one salon he estimated that there were fifty carpets, in each of four piles, and the two men standing by to turn the carpets back so that customers could examine the patterns and colours. He knew of at least twenty salons: that made over four thousand carpets – and obviously he had not seen all the storerooms.

Every time he went into a new place he glanced at the men waiting on duty.

Each time, he half-expected to see Cartwright; but he did not.

He saw a dozen places where a man might hide; small doors marked *Private,* others marked *Emergency Exit,* alcoves where rolled carpets were leaning, passages leading to every section of the warehouse. A man who knew this place well could slip from one section to another without the slightest difficulty, and remain hidden from twenty policemen; unless he had a slice of luck the only real hope of finding Cartwright would be by having a search warrant, ordering everyone to stand where they were, and making a kind of military operation of the search. It might come to that: West wouldn't give up if he thought there was a real chance of getting Cartwright.

He kept catching glimpses of Evans and the policewoman. Then he followed his blonde along a narrow passage, and she said calmly: "This actually goes underneath the road, sir, the underground premises extend much further than the ones above. Is this your first visit to London?"

"I've been here before," Gibson told her, and glanced over his shoulder.

No one was in sight.

He saw no need to feel uneasy, yet in a way he did. Evans, a man on the short side of medium height and with a thin face and very thin nose, was unmistakable; and Evans would not fall down on his job. They would probably meet again soon. The girl's ridiculous heels went tap-tap-tap on the cement floor of the tunnel, which was well lit. He saw more carpets at the far end, and brighter lights. He stepped through into another huge salon. Here were the British-made carpets, Axminster and Wilton, in great piles, some of them draped.

The uneasy feeling remained.

He told himself that there was no need for it, that nothing could possibly go wrong. He was not a nervous man, either and there was no need for nerves. *There couldn't be.* The girl was so normal, tap-tap-tapping and wriggle-wriggle-wriggling along.

Then Gibson saw Roy Cartwright.

Gibson had given up hope of seeing his quarry. Like all men who worked at speed, Roger West made a lot of bad guesses, and this had seemed likely to prove one of them. But there was Cartwright, standing behind a stack of carpets which were knee high to him, gaping, mouth open, as if he could not believe his eyes. Recognition was instantaneous, and it seemed to paralyse Cartwright. Gibson, recovering from the momentary shock, saw the puzzled way in which the girl looked from him to Cartwright and back. She didn't speak. Another man, small and elderly and with a humped back, was standing in a corner, head twisted round on his short neck, equally aware of the tension.

Gibson fell back on the obvious formalities.

"Good-afternoon, Mr Cartwright." Cartwright didn't answer. "I wonder if you will come to Mr Maddison's office with me?" That would not mean much to either the girl or the man with the humped back.

Cartwright still didn't answer.

"Is everything all right?" asked the blonde girl.

"Perfectly all right," Gibson told her. He was now using his normal speaking voice, and realised that it was a mistake; but he found what he had come for, the time for pretence should be over. "I want to see Mr Maddison at once. Come along, Mr Cartwright."

"You realise who Mr Cartwright *is,* don't you?" said the girl shrilly.

"Yes, Miss Osborn. Now, Mr Cartwright, you'll come along to the office with me, won't you?"

Gibson was suffering from his own shortcomings, then; from the fact that the only approach he could make when dealing with a situation like this was the formal one. He had learned his job thoroughly, but in many ways parrot-like; only when he had mastered it had his mind began to move outside the strait-jacket of rule and regulation, formal charge and formal answer.

Cartwright moved towards a corner of the pile of carpets and towards Gibson, as if resignedly, but Gibson did not like the expression in his eyes. Gibson jumped up on to the carpets and darted towards one of the tunnels.

The man with the humped back grabbed a corner of the top carpet and heaved, to fling a part of the carpet back. It rose like a great wave from the sea. Gibson saw it, tried to jump over it, but it caught him just above the ankle, and he was moving at such speed that he could not save himself from falling. He did not hurt himself, the carpets were so soft, but his legs were caught up in the top one and he could not keep himself free.

"Come back there!" he roared. "Come back!"

He was trying to get up, but something struck him behind the knees. He pitched forward. He knew that the other side of the carpet had been flicked over deliberately. Part of it was beneath him, part of it now covered his legs up to the knees. It was very heavy. He tried to kick it off, but could not get free. He caught a glimpse of Cartwright disappearing, and of the man with the hunched back holding the corner of another carpet, beneath the top one. The man's forearms were bare, and for the first time Gibson saw how the muscles stood out, and realised what great strength there was in those arms.

"Stop that man!" he roared.

The little man heaved, and the second carpet came up at Gibson. It was like another wave from a sea of carpets, and he couldn't save himself from it. The more he kicked and struggled, the more difficult it would be to get away. He had to keep still, had to make this man and the girl realise what they were doing. But it was difficult to be dignified; he was treading carpets like a man treading water where thick mud oozed beneath it.

He stopped moving, prepared to get out the best way he could, while he shouted: "In the name of the law, I demand—"

Something struck him on the back of the head. The weapon was heavy but soft, and it sent him forward again, on his knees. Before he realised what was happening, he felt a great weight and saw abysmal darkness descend upon him. A whole carpet. It was thick, the smell of wool and oily canvas was overpowering. Dust got into his mouth and caught at his throat, and he choked. In that moment he fought desperately, as. a drowning man, but all he could do was punch the thick pile, which seemed to press upon him, head to foot. He was aware of movement. He knew he was being pushed about; then realised that he was being rolled up in the carpet. He went over and over, and the dust was thick in his throat and nostrils; he began to cough. He could not stop. He could not put his hand to his face, or hold his stomach, or do anything to stop the paroxysm. It got worse. He was still being rolled over and over and over again. He was just aware of that, but the most awful thing was the coughing, because he seemed to be suffocating himself.

He was choking.

God! He must stop; he was choking to death, he just could not breathe. He couldn't breathe any air, it was all thick, clinging dust, parching his throat and tongue, filling his windpipe. He simply could not breathe. He was still coughing, and retching at the same time, but his eyes were streaming with tears of pain, his chest hurt, his throat hurt.

The rolling movement stopped.

He tried to hold his breath, but could not. He fought to stifle the coughing a little and succeeded, but he did not stop altogether. The pressure at his mouth and nose and eyes, as well as the pressure on his body and his chest, were all too great to bear. If he didn't get free soon, he would be suffocated to death.

Like the babies in their cots.

Chapter Nine

Hide and Seek

The blonde was standing by the entrance to the room, mouth agape, eyes rounded as if with horror. The humpbacked man was rolling the carpet over at one end, another man was rolling it in the middle, where it was a little bulkier.

"Wh—what are you doing, Mr Corrissey?" the girl gasped. "You'll suffocate him to death. He—he won't be able to breathe."

"He—he'll be all right," the hunchback said breathlessly. "I had to give Mr Cartwright a chance to escape. Don't you worry."

"You've got to let that man out of there," the girl exclaimed.

The hunchback stood back from the carpet. His assistant was standing and staring at him, as if expecting to be told what to do. The girl's breathing had become very harsh. Roy Cartwright had gone, and she had not seen where. There was silence all about them, except in this big room.

"You've got to let him out!" the girl screamed.

"Don't you worry, Miss Osborn," the hunchback said. He had sharp features and a thin face, and his head was held a little on one side; his chin was thrust forward, and pointed. "We're hiding him for an hour or two, that's all." He pushed his hand through bushy hair, and then stepped towards her, quite casually.

Something in his manner scared her. She sprang back, and turned round. Her spike heels bent over, and she staggered. Corrissey leapt at her. She knew that he was near and that she could not escape him, and she screamed again. He snatched a small carpet from a shelf and flung it over her. It dropped in front of her face and fell over her head, muffling the scream. She swayed, and tried to turn round. Corrissey reached her and flung his great arms round her, holding the carpet tight about her body, his thick, muscly arms encircling her completely. The other man came hurrying.

"Take her feet, Bert," Corrissey gasped.

The man bent down and lifted her feet off the ground. They carried her between them, like a sack, the man with the humped back obviously finding it awkward.

"Where—where we going to take her?" the other man demanded.

"Stockroom."

"But—"

"Get a move on!"

They carried the girl past the rolled carpet on the floor. There was no movement in it, as there had been. They went out, leaving the room empty. Except for their movements there was still no sound. They went awkwardly along a narrow passage, and Bert kicked open a door marked: *Private*. It was dark beyond.

"Put on a light," Corrissey ordered.

"Just—just a minute."

"Why don't you get a move on? We won't have long."

The second man let the girl's legs go with one arm, and groped for the switch. Lights went on in a small room, with many cubicles round the walls; rather like a wine cellar. Each bin was filled with pieces of carpet, pieces of wool, tools, tape, stores of all kinds. They went at the double. The girl was writhing and twisting, but hardly a sound was coming from the carpet. They turned a corner at the end of the lane between the bins, and Bert said gaspingly: "She'll be suffocated."

"You should worry about her."

"She didn't—"

"She saw what happened, didn't she?"

"Joe, listen! You can't—"

"I'm not going to put her away, but we've got to make sure she won't open her mouth too soon," said Corrissey. He held the girl's head and shoulders against his chest. "Let her go."

The other man lowered the girl's feet to the floor. Joe pushed her, so that she was standing on her own two feet, without support. She swayed. He stopped her from falling, supported her with one hand, and then flipped off the rug. The strength in his arms was astonishing, and the heavy rug was handled as if it were a sheet.

The blonde's hair was all mussed up and sticking out at both sides. She was covered in dust, over her hair, her face, her black suit. Her eyes were flickering, her mouth was wide open as she breathed in; each breath seemed to make her shudder.

"Get me some of that tape," Corrissey ordered.

Bert moved quickly enough now, and came back with a ball of backing tape, two inches wide. Corrissey twisted some round the girl's face, so that she couldn't call out, and now she heaved for breath, for she could only breathe through her nostrils. The bigger man looked scared. Corrissey cut off a length of tape, and twisted it round her wrists dexterously, as he sometimes tied rolled carpets and rugs. She swayed against him. *"Hold her, can't you?"* he said viciously. "Don't let her fall while I do her ankles." He bent down. In thirty seconds her ankles were tied, and she looked like a mummy not yet swathed. Now he lifted her over his shoulder, and carried her along the end passage. At a bin filled with webbing, he stopped, and said: "Take some of those rolls out." He waited, glancing over his shoulder, while the man obeyed, then hoisted the girl in. The bin was too shallow for her to lie at full length, but he pushed her so that her knees were bent and she was doubled up. "Stack those rolls round her," he ordered, "and then come back."

"Joe, you know I've always had a soft spot for her, I don't want—"

"Bert, do what I tell you!" Corrissey swung round and sped towards the door, making very little noise. He stepped out of the storeroom into the passage. There was no sound except of his movements. He reached the big room where Gibson was rolled up in the carpet, went straight to that carpet and kicked at it until it was flat against a wall. Then he rolled up carpet after carpet from the pile on which Gibson had been standing, working with furious energy. Each one he rolled against the wall, so that the one where Gibson lay helplessly was hidden by a little pyramid of rolled carpets. He drew back, wiping his wet forehead with his arm, and stood taking in deep breaths.

He heard footsteps; and voices.

Then Bert came out of the storeroom.

"Fixed it?"

"No one can see her, but she can't stay there long. That's definite."

"She won't. You needn't worry, Bert," Corrissey said placatingly. "Keep your mouth shut if anyone comes and asks questions. Leave the talking to me."

"You bet I will," Bert muttered. He had a broad, round face, and rather dull eyes, which seemed frightened and resentful. There was something of the look of a cretin about him, but his body was upright and strong, and his rolled sleeves showed that the muscles of his arms were almost as strong as the hump-backed man's. There had been many times when Bert's look of imbecility had fooled the police completely; and if he did what he was told, it would again.

A man and a woman came hurrying, and one of the store's salesmen was just behind them. The man was tall, thin-faced and angry-looking; the woman, in her thirties, had an anxious and yet kindly look.

"Has anyone been through here in the past five minutes?" the thin-faced man demanded.

Corrissey said: "There was a man, five or six minutes ago, sir."

"Where did he go?"

"He went back, sir."

"If he'd gone back, we should have seen him," the thin-faced man said, and he took a card out of his pocket and thrust it into Corrissey's face. "I'm from Scotland Yard. The man I'm looking for is Inspector Gibson." Then he flashed: "Have you seen Mr Roy Cartwright today?"

"No, sir," Corrissey lied, smoothly.

"I'm sorry, Inspector Evans," said the salesman, "but I do assure you that anyone could have left here and taken any one of several turnings. That's what will have happened to your colleague. It is a very elaborate system of salons, and—"

"Mind if I look?" asked Evans.

"You must please yourself, sir," the salesman said, "but—"

"If you find anyone down here, I'll put five pounds into your hands," said Corrissey. He spoke quietly and vehemently and with such apparent conviction that the salesman smiled, and Bert nodded and looked vacant. Evans and the woman with him seemed to hesitate, before Evans said: "We'll look, all the same." He swung round on Bert. "Have you seen Mr Cartwright?"

"Mr who, sir?" Bert looked startled.

"Cartwright."

"I dunno know anyone of that name."

"You know, Bert, the young Boss," Corrissey said, as if reasoning with a child, and Bert's eyes lit up.

"Oh. Mr Roy. No—no, sir, not today I haven't seen him."

"Did you see a tall man?"

"Y—y—y—yes, sir, like Joe says," Bert answered. "He went back the way he came."

There was nothing brilliant about Detective Inspector Evans and he was not, in fact, as sharp as he looked. His thin features and rather bright eyes, as well as his manner, gave the impression that he knew much more than he did, and he used this fact skilfully. He was one of the really thorough and painstaking men at the Yard, and one day would become a superintendent by sheer doggedness and determination, and because he knew every rule in the book.

He was not convinced that Gibson had come here and gone back. They had last seen him ten minutes or so ago, and he had gone one way, the policewoman had gone the other. Neither of them had seen Gibson, but they had met at the passage leading to this section of the underground storerooms.

Two years ago there had been a great deal of carpet stealing, especially Persian and Indian carpets of great value. Three warehouses up and down the country had dealt in these stolen goods, but it had been difficult to identify each carpet and rug.

Evans had worked for nearly twelve months before he had found the warehouse he was looking for. Carpets had been unloaded at the docks, loaded into delivery vans, which had switched destination; a simple method which might have gone on for years.

The one thing that Evans had discovered during that case was the high repute of Maddison Brothers. No one had a word to say against them, and there had not been the slightest hint that the firm had been involved.

He also knew these storerooms and salesrooms; they had been searched several times. And as far as he knew, none of the staff or the management had lied to him.

Margaret Webb, the policewoman, had stood aside during all this, but when he went forward she followed him and watched the two warehousemen. Neither of them showed any expression, and the blankness on the face of the bigger man was almost imbecilic. Evans went to the rolled-up carpets immediately, and stood looking down at them. Some were thick and some were thin, as if they were of different sizes. All were rolled up so that they were absolutely even at each end, one or two were a little uneven. He kicked at the top ones with the heel of his right foot, but made little or no impression; they hardly moved.

"Like me to unroll them?" inquired Corrissey, and there was no doubt of the sarcasm in his voice.

"I might do," Evans said; he was always a man it was easy to rile. "Isn't the storeroom along here?"

"Yes, sir," the salesman said, and he was glaring at Corrissey. "If you would like to examine it, you are very welcome."

"If it's all the same to you, Inspector, me and my mate will get on with our work," said Corrissey. "We've got a dozen more carpets to roll and move down to dispatch in the next hour. We've lost enough time as it is."

"I've no intention of stopping you from working," Evans said tartly.

He led the way to the storeroom. The salesman followed, and Maggie Webb glanced round at the warehousemen. The foolish-looking one was staring after them, the sharp-faced and sharp-witted Corrissey was already bending down over the corner of the pile of carpets.

"Get a move on, Bert," he ordered.

"Okay, okay, I'm working, aren't I?" Bert asked, and he was almost sullen.

They began to roll carpets.

Evans went into the storeroom. The bins were all too shallow to hide a man, and he did not look into any of them, only along the passages. He sent Maggie one way, while he went the other; again they met near the door, and the uneasy salesman.

"There really isn't anywhere else he can be," the salesman said. "I do assure you that you must have missed him."

Evans grunted.

But there was nothing more he could do, and he went back to the room where the hunchback and his assistant were rolling and tying carpets. The hunchback was intent on his work; the other man kept looking round, but there was no reason at all why the policeman should suspect anything but curiosity.

The party of three disappeared.

Corrissey stopped working, and wiped his forehead again; for the first time he looked nervous. Bert was trembling, and looking at the pile of carpets.

"What are you going to do with him?"

"He's going to stay there where he is until the heat's off," Corrissey answered. "The police are searching all the vans when they get round the corner, but they won't keep that up for long now. As soon as they stop, we'll get this load to the docks. I can lay it on."

"Joe—"

"Bert, you don't have to string along," said the humpbacked man, "but if you know which side your bread's buttered, you will. I know what I'm doing."

Bert said in a mild voice: "Okay, Joe, but Miss Osborn will be all right now, won't she?"

"You leave her to me. I'll see that nothing happens to her," Corrissey said. "It's all laid on, Bert. You just keep your mouth shut and do what you're told, and you'll be set up for life. Okay?"

"Okay."

"That's the boy," Corrissey said, and clapped the other on the shoulder. He treated Bert much as a man might treat a backward child. "Now how about knocking off for a draw?"

Bert's eyes lit up.

Corrissey took out a packet of cigarettes, proffered them, and then lit up for them both. He sat on a corner of the pile of carpets, looking at the rolled-up carpets, where there was no sign of movement or of life.

Chapter Ten

Puzzle

Roger looked up as Evans entered his office, waved to a chair, and then went on speaking into the telephone to AS Division. There was no news yet of the missing Lee child, and the father hadn't yet been traced. Ledbetter was trying to force the pace at the Yard, and Roger did not blame him.

"We won't miss a trick," he assured the Divisional man. "I'll come over as soon as I've got through the chores here."

"Looking for Cartwright?"

"That's the main chore."

"Well, I hope you soon get him," Ledbetter said, and forebore to add that it was a pity that the man had ever been allowed to go free. Roger rang off. Evans was sitting on the edge of his chair, as always; he was a nervous type when dealing with superiors, a little too anxious to impress.

"Well, Evans, what've you got?" asked Roger. He did not need telling that in fact Evans and Gibson had drawn a blank; Gibson would have sent word otherwise.

"As far as I could judge there was no sign of Cartwright at the Maddison warehouse," Evans answered, with great deliberation, "but a peculiar thing happened, sir."

"How peculiar?"

"Gibson left before I had an opportunity of reporting to him."

The difficult thing was to conceal a smile. Gibson might look ponderous compared with this man, but in fact could move twice as fast.

"Was he on to something?"

"I simply don't know," Evans admitted, and made it obvious that he felt slighted; he would probably have behaved differently if he had known that Gibson had recommended him to this job. "We combed the salesrooms and the warehouse through, and then Police Officer Webb and I lost him."

"Lost?"

"I could have sworn he would be in the end storeroom, where the Axminsters and Wiltons are kept," Evans said. "He wasn't there, though. I made quite sure, just in case anything had happened to him."

"What would?" demanded Roger. This was so unexpected that it was difficult to grasp quickly.

Evans said: "I know it doesn't make much sense, but I can't understand how we missed him. Still, he wasn't there. A chap at the door said that he left before us. Can't understand it," Evans went on. "Have you heard from him?"

"Not yet," Roger said. "He'll turn up with some news soon."

"We might have been more successful if he had kept me informed," Evans said, and thus betrayed his real frame of mind: he was sore.

"Did he give you any idea at all where he was going?"

"None at all."

"Positive that Cartwright's not at the warehouse?"

"If he were ever there, he got word that we were on the premises and pushed off," Evans said.

"He wasn't picked up," Roger remarked uneasily. He had been wrong to let Cartwright go in the first place; no one would blame him, but the fact remained. Had he also been wrong not to get a search warrant for the warehouse? He tried to be rational. This report was puzzling, but hardly sensational. It looked as if Gibson had gone off on a line that he didn't want Evans to follow. As soon as he had news worth reporting, he would telephone. But was that really being rational? Could anything have happened to Gibson?

"What would you do if you had your own way?" he asked, and realised that he was really passing the buck. One wrong decision had got under his skin, and he mustn't let it remain.

"Wait for Gibson to deign to report, I suppose," Evans said tartly.

Another time that attitude would have annoyed Roger; now he ignored it, and said briskly: "He might, but I'd like to make sure that warehouse is properly searched now, and to check on all the vans. I'll fix the warrant. You lay on the men, will you?"

That was giving Evans a measure of authority, and he brightened immediately.

Roger got the warrant signed by the Assistant Commissioner in ten minutes, and the search had begun in twenty; but there was no sign of Cartwright and none of Gibson anywhere.

When that report came in, Roger pushed his chair back and glowered at the wall. It was almost as if there were a jinx on him, and he could not do the right thing. If Cartwright had been at the warehouse then he, Roger, had probably scared him away when talking to Maddison. If Gibson was in danger—

Nonsense.

Was it?

There was no point in brooding, anyhow, but plenty in checking everything he had left undone. He mustn't make any more mistakes.

He could have sworn that Maddison had been quite sure that Cartwright had not committed suicide, and there was still no report of a body having been found in the Thames. He hadn't been out to see Maddison's wife. That job should have been done before – and he had been wrong to earmark that for himself instead of asking the Surrey police to fix it. It would have to be done quickly now. He could still get there before Maddison got home.

Another thought nagged at him. If he had gone to Maddison's London premises, would he be missing? Had he sent Gibson into a trap?

Uneasy and glum, Roger looked up as the door opened, and Commander Hardy came in. Hardy was short and very broad, well-dressed, quiet-voiced, one of the Yard's good brains, who had a gift for administration which had put him in his present post, second only to the Assistant Commissioner in the C.I.D. His grey hair was cut short; he had a fresh, scrubbed look. Roger stood up.

"Sit down," Hardy said casually. "Is anything in about Cartwright?"

"Nothing useful. Gibson's gone haring off, and hasn't reported. I don't know where he is."

"On to something, if I know Gibson." That was a reassuringly normal reaction. "Anything found at the warehouse or in those vans?"

"Nothing."

"The Civil Commissioner's been beefing," Hardy confided. "Apparently traffic's worse than usual today, and we're making it even worse than the usual rush hour. Can you—"

"I've fixed it."

Hardy grinned. "Anticipated the request, as usual."

Roger said uneasily: "I'm not feeling so pleased with myself, skipper." He explained why, and went on: "I've got off on the wrong foot, and can't get back."

"When you pick Cartwright up, you'll forget you ever felt like that," Hardy said briskly. "Do you think he killed these babies?"

"I don't know yet. He could have. I can't get any proof that he was out at all on Friday evening – but I can't prove he didn't go out about the time the Shaw child was killed, either."

"At heart you don't think he did, do you?"

"The explanation looks too easy," Roger answered. "There's something about the case that I don't get. This Maddison baby threat makes it vendetta-ish, too." He grinned. "I know! I said I couldn't get anything right." A telephone rang, almost at his hand, and he picked up the receiver quickly. "West here."

"I'll be seeing you," said Hardy.

"Just had a call from AS Division," the speaker said on the telephone. "They've found the man Lee and his child, but—"

Roger's eyes lit up.

"Something to make you change your mind?" asked Hardy from the door.

"But what?" asked Roger into the telephone.

"Lee's got his child up on a roof, and says that he'll jump down with it if we won't let him have possession of the child. Mr Ledbetter wants to know if—"

"Tell him I'm on my way; I'll talk to him by radio," Roger said, and banged down the receiver as Hardy, startled by the different tone in his voice, looked in again from the open door. Then he grinned. If there was one thing likely to jolt Roger West out of his present mood, it was action: and obviously he was going to get some.

Roger flicked on the radio as he drove out of the Yard, and when Information answered, he said brusquely: "Advise Mr Ledbetter to promise this man anything, anything at all."

"Right, sir."

It would take half an hour to get to Ealing Common, Roger realised, and any moment word might come that the father, obviously deranged, had actually carried out his threat. Roger did not need to tell Information to advise him the moment there was any news; they would pick him up on the instant. He could not be sure that rushing to Ealing would help much, but he had to be on the go; action of any kind would quieten his feeling of unease.

Yet it meant putting off the call on Maddison's wife again. Was that another mistake?

The man named Bert, alone in the packing room for ten minutes, walked quickly towards the storeroom, slipped inside and, with the light switched on, hurried towards the bin where Helen Osborn had been left. When he reached it, he stood staring, smiling, then he eased her bonds. She was unconscious, but alive. He lifted her out of the bin, grunting, and was about to take her towards the dispatch room when Corrissey arrived.

"What the hell are you doing?" he demanded. "She could get us twenty years inside! Put her back."

Bert stood holding the girl, while Corrissey nearly spat at him.

"Put her back! I won't hurt her. I've got to pay her to keep quiet, but that'll come later. Put her back!"

Bert turned round and did so; and noticed that Corrissey was sweating.

Bingley Court consisted of a block of small flats, not far from Ealing Common. They were fairly modern, and looked squat and unattractive against the bright skyline. The walls were of plain grey cement and the windows were all square and small. Houses in the surrounding streets were old-fashioned and built mostly in terraces, which made the block of flats look even more incongruous.

People were already hurrying there.

Roger saw a fire engine drawing up in the middle of a road which had been cordoned off by the police. A turntable had been run up, and two men were standing on the platform. He hooted at a dozen people thronging the road, and they scattered, to let him pass. A policeman recognised him as he pulled up.

"Park my car for me, will you?" Roger said, as he got out.

"Yes, sir."

"Anything developed?"

"He's still up there, sir."

Roger hurried round the corner, and saw Ledbetter standing and talking with a fireman wearing a steel helmet. Most people were staring up at the roof; there was a noisy cackle of voices. Windows had been flung open up and down the street; men and women were leaning out of them.

Two people were standing at the top of a house opposite Bingley Court holding on to a chimney stack.

Ledbetter saw Roger, and came hurrying.

"Any luck?" Roger asked.

Ledbetter growled: "He's crazy as a coot. He's blocked the only way up to the roof, it will take hours to cut a way through, and he says he won't come down until he sees his wife, and she promises him he can keep the child. Hell of a job," Ledbetter added, "and God knows what will happen to that kid."

"We've got to get the child down," Roger said. "Have you promised him—"

"Promised him the earth and the moon," answered Ledbetter. "He may be crazy over the baby but he's no fool otherwise. He knows we'll promise anything, and the moment he's let us have the child, it won't mean a thing. He seems to think that if the wife will promise, he'll be all right."

Roger said slowly: "She's been told?"

"No."

"I'll go and tell her," Roger said, "and I'll probably bring her here."

Ledbetter said: "I thought that's what you'd try. Got Cartwright yet?"

"No."

"I've been thinking," Ledbetter said. "I've been asking myself if Cartwright would have come rushing to the place like he did last night if he had killed that kid. Funny thing, ever since we found that MG of his I've been wondering more about it. Chap might be a psycho, but he'd know it. Can't see him committing suicide. He'd be more likely to take advantage of being mental – these days especially. He knows he'd almost certainly get a guilty but insane verdict, and be looked after in hospital for a few years. I'm beginning to wonder if you were right, after all."

Roger smiled.

"Best bit of news I've had today! Tell Lee that I've gone for his wife, won't you?"

"I'll broadcast it right away," Ledbetter promised, and as Roger drove off a minute later, he could hear Ledbetter's voice going over a police loudspeaker.

He had no doubt that Mrs Lee would come here; but would her husband believe her, if she gave the promise that he wanted? And what could give a man, so distraught as Lee, the faith that he could trust his wife?

Did Maddison's wife trust him?

Presumably not, if she had gone to the police against his wishes, or even without his knowledge.

"I had to tell the police. I know you said we didn't want a fuss, but I had to tell them," Maddison's wife said. She was looking at her child, asleep in a pram inside the hall of the lovely house at Esher, and then she looked up at her husband, her eyes glistening, and cried: "If anything happened to baby, I would kill myself!"

"But nothing will, my darling," Maddison soothed. "And I think you were right to do what you did. The police are watching now; he's doubly safe. There's nothing to worry about at all.

Chapter Eleven

Rooftop

A middle-aged woman, obviously Mrs Lee's mother, opened the door to Roger at Ealing. She stood squarely in front of it, as if she were used to barring the path to anyone who wanted to get in, and said flatly: "Mrs Lee has nothing to say, and can see no one."

"I'm Superintendent West," Roger said briskly. "We've found the baby and want your daughter's help."

The woman dropped back.

"You've *found* him?" Her eyes, so cold and hostile a moment before, lit up as with a great blaze of light. She swung round, and Roger grabbed her arm.

"Don't tell her yet."

The mother swung round again, a tall woman, heavy-figured but very light on her feet; and now her fine eyes carried a different light: of sharp anxiety.

"He's all right, isn't he?"

"Perfectly all right," Roger answered. "Mr Lee has him on the roof of a block of flats, and threatens to throw himself and the child over unless Mrs Lee promises to let him have custody. He won't listen to the police, and he might carry out his threat. Do you think your daughter is strong enough to face him?"

The mother said in a whisper: "She'll have to be. Of course she will be."

Roger followed her upstairs. The carpet deadened the sound of his footsteps, and he realised more clearly than before that this was the house of much wealthier people than Mrs Kindle and her absent husband, more like the Maddisons. The woman with him was breathing very hard, as if a little frightened of the effect that this news would have upon her daughter.

"Charlotte," she called, as they approached the room where Roger had seen Mrs Lee before. "Mr West thinks that you can help with …"

There was a flurry of footsteps, and the door swung open. Mrs Lee stood looking at him, clutching the door, very pale, eyes glistening, as if she were still in the grip of hysteria. She might well be; and if this new shock set her screaming again, there would be little left to be done. Was there a way to steady her? The mother obviously intended to leave it to him, and that was probably wise. He prayed for the right words.

"Have you found him?" she demanded in a taut voice.

Roger said, very quietly: "Mrs Lee, it rests in your hands whether we can save your child or not."

She caught her breath; that was all. The wildness was still in her eyes; it would not surprise him if she flung her arms above her head and began to shout and scream when he told her the truth.

"Your husband has the child, and is threatening to kill himself and the child unless you promise to let him have the full custody."

She gasped: "But I can't!"

"Charlotte," her mother began, and then broke off.

"I haven't any doubt that you will have custody of the child when all this is over," Roger said, "but there's only one way to stop your husband from carrying out his threat. That is to make him think you'll let him have the child. You'll have to convince him that you mean it, Mrs Lee. Will you come and do that?"

If she broke down now, it would be all over.

"Charlotte," her mother said again, and stopped; she was much more nuisance than help.

"Where—where are they?" Mrs Lee asked.

"Not far away. On the roof of Bingley Court."

"On the *roof*—" Mrs Lee began, and suddenly buried her face in her hands. She was not quite normal, of course; that might be the result of the tension between her and her husband, the result of months and possibly years of strain. Could she get a hold on herself now? And could she carry the task through if once she started?

She raised her head and lowered her hands.

"I'll come at once," she said.

On the way, Roger talked a little; enough to tell them both what to expect. The mother sat behind, Mrs Lee by his side. Twice he checked with Information that the situation hadn't changed. Once, Information said: "There is no report from Mr Gibson, sir."

That was Roger's first bad moment since he had been here; he was beginning to feel really worried about Gibson. But there was little more he could do.

"Put another call round to the Divisions and ask them to step up the search for him."

"Very good, sir."

Mrs Lee was saying, almost to herself: "I must make him believe me. I must." Roger was staring straight ahead, and thinking, not of her and the immediate problem, but of Gibson. Had he been in that warehouse? There was little doubt that Edward Maddison had known something about Cartwright's movements, and was sure that he had not committed suicide. Had Gibson got on to Cartwright through Maddison? Maddison was certainly worth following up; his type often broke down completely if they were pressed hard enough. He ought to have kept his mind clear for that particular job, Roger thought, not come tearing along here to make a hero of himself. What made him think he was the only man at the Yard who could handle this Lee job? The truth was, he had been side-tracked because a baby was involved. It was almost an obsession to make sure that no more died of violence.

"Shake out of it!" he told himself.

"… must make him believe me," Mrs Lee was saying. Then in a louder voice: "How long will it be? Why aren't you hurrying?"

"In less than five minutes we'll be there," Roger assured her. He must get his mind off Gibson and the other job; now that he was here, he must try to help this woman.

"How long have you been separated from your husband, Mrs Lee?"

"About—about six months."

So they parted two months after the child had been born.

"Are you sueing for divorce?"

"Yes," Mrs Lee answered, in a muffled voice.

"Why?"

"I really don't see—" began the mother.

"Oh, it doesn't matter," Mrs Lee said. "Harry was—well, there was a girl at the office. He said that he would give her up, but he didn't. I couldn't stand thinking that he was with her, while I was at home with the baby; I simply couldn't stand it."

"No woman could be expected to stand it," interpolated the mother.

Roger thought: "Ah." He turned a corner without speaking, and saw the first of the crowds. The mother's inflexible tone of voice told him much that he wanted to know. The young wife was living with her parents, in a good home, and under the older woman's domination; probably she had been for a long time. "No woman could be expected to stand it." Well, countless women had. How much of this trouble between husband and wife was due to maternal influence?

Roger stopped as they reached the corner. A policeman leaned forward and opened the door and helped Mrs Lee out. Immediately, she broke into a run. Roger got out quickly and ran after her, but policemen were blocking her path; she couldn't go far. Roger caught her arm. The older woman was a long way behind, and would not find it easy to catch up.

"What we have to do," Roger said, "is to go up on a turntable and talk to your husband. Do heights worry you?"

"No." Mrs Lee was peering upwards desperately, hoping to catch a glimpse of her husband and the child, but there was no hope of doing that from here. They reached the fire escape; the turntable was being lowered and another one had been brought up, so that there were two of them. Mrs Lee kept staring upwards; she did everything she was told without speaking but without loss of a moment. Soon, she and Roger were standing on a turntable and being raised, very slowly. The street fell away beneath them, the people in it getting smaller and smaller. There was a hush, as if everyone below was holding his breath. The grey-white surface of the building was very near them. Faces appeared at many of the windows and eyes were glistening or shining. Roger stood with his arm round the woman's waist, knowing that she hardly realised where she was; the only thing that mattered for her was to see her child. They went up and up even more slowly, and the people below looked like midgets now.

A voice on a loudspeaker boomed. "Mr Lee, your wife is on her way up to you. Can you hear us?"

There was no answer.

Now Roger could see the guttering. In a few seconds, they would be raised above the level of the roof and would see the man. Mrs Lee was quivering slightly, partly because she was holding herself very still. A breeze blew a lock of hair across her eyes, and she shifted it with a jerky movement.

They rose above the level of the roof and saw Lee standing some way back, still clutching the child.

The turntable was within six feet of the guttering; six feet which were unbridgable until they were moved towards the roof itself. He saw the man, a youngish man who was nearly bald, dressed in a dark grey suit.

The child in his arms seemed to be asleep.

The man's eyes were glittering, and he was staring only at his wife. He did not move, but called out in a clear, carrying voice: "If we can't live with you, we're not going to live at all."

So that was it: Lee hoped to blackmail his wife into breaking off divorce proceedings. Sane or mad made little difference; he knew exactly what he was doing.

"I mean it," Harry Lee said.

"I know you do," responded Charlotte Lee, and she spoke more calmly than Roger had yet heard her. "You mustn't hurt baby, though. Put him down."

"It isn't any use," retorted Lee, quite flatly. "If you won't take me back, you can't have Richard. You've got to come back with us, Charlotte. And it's no use to lie to me; I always know when you lie."

There was no sense in this; no easy way out; no real hope. Whether the cause was the mother, down below, or whether it was the girl in the office, or whether there were other causes which went much deeper, Roger did not know. He recognised stalemate here. He had an impression of great stubbornness; the mother would not give way, the father would not give way, and there was no meeting-place for them.

The turntable was swaying slightly, a little nearer the roof. Roger was judging the distance. At four feet, he would risk jumping, but he would be happier if he could have only two. He had to make a standing jump, and wasn't sure how the turntable would react; in fact a fireman ought to be up here, to leap on to the roof and take Lee by surprise.

The firemen were on the other turntable, two or three yards away. He knew that they were going to make a leap for it the moment it seemed safe. First concentrate the man's attention on his wife, and then swing the second turntable nearer so that the firemen could get to him. Rescuing the baby was not the problem now; the real tragedy lay in what this would do to the parents.

Then Mrs Lee wrenched herself free from him, and leapt towards the roof.

She had been standing very still, trembling slightly; the calmness of her voice had seemed to declare that she knew that she must try to reason with her husband, had given no indication of what was in her mind. Now, before Roger could stop her, she jumped. He grabbed at her dress, and it slipped through his fingers.

The turntable swayed dangerously.

"Charlotte'." her husband screamed. *"Charlotte!"*

Chapter Twelve

Jump

Roger felt the swaying of the turntable, and staggered to one side. He saw the woman's outstretched hands reaching for the guttering. He knew that she hadn't a chance of saving herself. Her feet were still on the edge of the turntable, but there was no hope that she could recover her balance. Roger tried desperately to keep himself steady. Then he saw Lee rushing forward to try to save his wife. Oh, God. They would both fall.

Roger lurched and clutched the woman's ankles. He checked her fall, but did not think there was a chance of saving her. He heard men shouting, but could not distinguish what they said. He heard screaming from the street. He felt the woman's weight on his arms and shoulders; unless he let go, he would fall with her.

The weight actually eased a little.

Roger saw Lee, lying flat on the roof, arms outstretched, and holding his wife's wrists. She was stretched, as a bridge, between the roof and the turntable. Lee was staring down at her, wild-eyed.

Then a hand touched Roger's arm.

"Take it easy, sir," said one of the firemen from the other turntable. "Hold her until we get a bit closer. All ok now, sir."

Roger saw Lee, so far over the edge that it looked as if he were bound to fall, but his wife wasn't falling any more. There was much less strain on Roger's arms, too, and a sense of security rather than of danger. Then one of the firemen jumped on to the roof, other men appeared on it, and more escapes were run up. It was only a matter of seconds to safety for them all.

The baby lay still on the roof, where the father had put it. It began to cry.

The acute danger had lasted for perhaps sixty seconds. Roger, standing on the roof, felt as if he had been through an hour-long ordeal. He seemed to be swaying, as if he could never stop. He could see the turntable some distance from the roof, and the gap was so great that it looked like death even to think about leaping it.

The woman was lying on the roof, her husband on his knees beside her. A fireman was holding the crying baby.

Lee was in tears, too.

Charlotte Lee was crying.

Roger drove from Ealing at about half-past five that evening, deliberately going slowly and carefully. He hadn't thrown off the effect of those sixty seconds, but he had to soon, and driving would help him back to normal more quickly than anything else. He was alone, with the radio crackling, and calls going to and fro through the ether. Most of it was routine, but there were some comments about Gibson, who hadn't been found. It was damned queer about Gibson, and Roger tried to be rational about him again. Gibson was the old reliable, wasn't he? The last man to go haring off on his own so that he could get results in a lone wolf act. He wouldn't stick his neck out too far.

Roger turned into the Yard, and something in the alacrity with which a man jumped forward to open his door, and in the expression of the eyes of the sergeants on duty in the hall, told him that the story of the rooftop at Ealing had turned him into a hero again. If only they knew! He hurried along to his office, hoping against hope that there would be word of Gibson.

Evans was at his desk, looking round.

"Just brought my report, sir," he said, moving from the desk; there was something in the set of his chin which told Roger that he did not share the hero-worship; Evans had only one hero. "I can't help thinking that it's most peculiar."

"About Gibson?"

"I could swear that either Miss Webb or I would have seen him coming out of that dispatch room."

"But you know he wasn't there."

"As a matter of fact—" began Evans, and then broke off.

He had something on his mind, Roger knew; and probably something on his conscience – as he, Roger, felt guilty because he still hadn't seen Maddison's wife. Roger moved to his chair and sat down, lifted a telephone and said: "Have someone send me up some tea and sandwiches – for two." The 'for two' obviously mollified Evans. "Sit down," he said to Evans, and wished he could think of some way of postponing this session for a while. He ought to have looked in at home on the way from Ealing. He hadn't, because Janet would know in a moment that he had been badly shaken. "Let's have it," he went on, and offered cigarettes.

"I don't smoke, thanks," Evans said; of course he didn't. "As a matter of fact, I'm not sure I didn't miss something pretty serious."

"What kind of thing?"

"Well," Evans began, and gulped; this weighed heavy on his conscience all right, and that meant that 'serious' was the operative word. "I've been trying to think how I would hide a body."

Roger actually shouted. *"What?"*

"I know," said Evans, "that's how it affected me when I first thought of it, and it really shook me. But it's no use blinking at facts, is it? Maggie and me didn't see Gibson come out, and we've got eyes at the back of our heads. The more I think of it, the more positive I am that he didn't come out of that packing and storage department. I've had a long talk with Maggie, and I've spoken in person to every one of our chaps who was watching the doors. None of them saw Gibson. He might have slipped one or two of them, but that's all."

"I see what you mean," Roger said. He felt a tightening of the muscles at the back of his neck and at his mouth, more tension than he had yet known. "Well, where would you put a body?"

He could have answered without a word from Evans, who said: "Roll it up in a carpet."

If it took a man as long as that to reach an obvious conclusion, it was a poor show: but there was no point in telling Evans that now.

"Gibson's a big man," Roger temporised. "As big as I am. The carpet would look like a barrel."

"Not if it was one of those fat Indians, it wouldn't," said Evans. "I've been checking – I slipped into Simms Warehouse in the Strand; I've got a pal along there. We rolled a couple of chairs up in a carpet, big thick Mirzapore thing, fifteen feet by eighteen. It looked fat all right, but there wasn't much difference between the ends and the middle. Just looked like a bigger carpet than most, that's all. And"— Evans was moistening his lips—"I remember there was a fat carpet at the bottom of a pile they'd got all ready rolled up for shipping."

So that was the real cause of his feeling of guilt.

"There was time to get that carpet into a van before we started searching them," Evans went on gloomily. "They got him out all right. We'll find him in the river, as like as not – and Cartwright, I wouldn't wonder."

"We'll go over and have another look round," Roger decided, partly because that was what Evans was after, and partly because a second search might catch the staff at the warehouse unawares. "Come on."

The silvery-haired old man was at the counter, and looked startled when the two Yard men appeared.

"I'm afraid Mr Edward's gone, sir, but Mr Ramsbottom, the manager, is in, as it's our seven o'clock closing night. I'll call him ..."

Ramsbottom was small, thin, wiry; rather like a Yorkshire terrier.

"I don't know what it is you suspect, Superintendent, or what you expect to find this time, but as I told your men earlier, I'll give you all the help I can. You'll find nothing that you shouldn't here."

They still found no trace of Gibson or of Cartwright.

Ramsbottom told the police that Joe Corrissey had left at five o'clock, with Bert May, his assistant packer; only the showrooms opened until seven o'clock. The two men usually had a lift on a van going to the garage, which was at the company's dockside warehouse.

"Get after them, we want to talk to them quickly," Roger said to Evans. "I'll have a word with the dockside police now." He felt an increasing sense of frustration, because there was no body, and no evidence that Gibson had been killed or hidden in a carpet. Evans was obviously prepared to work all night, if needs be, and as obviously was frightened of what they might find.

"Did anything else unusual happen today?" Roger asked Ramsbottom.

"I can't think of anything."

"There was the girl who took Gibson round," Evans put in. "A tall blonde – where is she?"

"That would be Miss Osborn. She will have gone home," Ramsbottom answered. "The office staff goes at five o'clock; we only have a few salesmen and late shift workers on duty until seven o'clock."

"I'd like Miss Osborn's address, please."

It was after half-past six when Roger and Evans left Maddisons, with the feeling of frustration and disquiet deeper than ever. Roger called Ledbetter by radio; there was nothing new about the Kindle case, but Mrs Kindle was back home, with a sister staying with her. Mrs Lee was also back home, with her husband and the baby. The Maddisons were home. There was still no word about Gibson. Roger sent Evans to the dockside warehouse and to check on Corrissey and May, and went himself to the address of the blonde who had taken Gibson round the warehouse and salerooms. She lived in a small flatlet in Earl's Court, which she shared with a short, dark-haired girl who worked in a department of a Fleet Street newspaper. She hadn't come in yet.

Roger arranged for her friend to telephone the Yard as soon as the Osborn girl came back, and left two men watching the flat.

It was then seven o'clock.

He went back to the Yard. Hardy had left, and so had the Assistant Commissioner, and only the night duty men were in; the Yard had a forlorn kind of look. Evans reported almost at once that Corrissey was not at home, and that a general call was out for him. The assistant, Herbert May, lodged at Corrissey's home, and was there.

"Have you talked to May?" Roger asked.

"He simply says that Gibson went out of the department," answered Evans. "I can't get another word out of him. I know one thing, sir."

"What's that?"

"Corrissey wouldn't talk if he knew all there was to know, and I wouldn't trust him round the corner. But May is different. We could break him down all right."

"Step up the search for Corrissey, and talk to May," Roger said. "If you get anything at all, telephone me at Bell Street."

"I'll do that," promised Evans.

Roger left the Yard a little after seven thirty. The boys would be looking forward to seeing him, and the difficulty tonight would be to behave naturally with them; the disappearance of Gibson was like a cloud hanging over his head. His radio was silent as he drove. He felt almost guilty at driving this way, instead of towards the docks or out to Esher, but Evans, the Divisional and the Surrey people between them could do far more than he, and one thing was quite certain: he needed a break. Even a couple of hours, a good meal, and Janet and the boys for company, would make a world of difference.

He turned into Bell Street, a pleasant Chelsea thoroughfare with some detached and some semi-detached houses, all with small gardens beautifully tended, tulips and wallflowers in many of the beds, grass looking trim and neat, here and there a lawnmower clattering. As he drew near his own house, halfway along the street, he saw the car parked outside it, and recognised Spendlove's dark green Jaguar sports car. The last thing he wanted was a talk with the newspaperman, but Spendlove wasn't at the wheel, so Janet had asked him in, and if he thought it worth coming at all he would think it worth waiting for hours. The wise thing was to see what he wanted and get rid of him.

Roger pulled up in front of his garage, and saw Spendlove in the front room, Scoopy standing by him, and Richard near and doubled up with laughter. The newspaperman had made a conquest there.

But why had he come?

Chapter Thirteen

Uneasy Night

"... and when he opened the envelope he found a card which said: 'Don't buy, beg or steal cigarettes'," Spendlove was saying as Roger opened the door. Richard was gurgling with laughter, Scoopy was smiling. "I was just telling your youngsters about methods of stopping smoking," Spendlove said. He looked clear-eyed and was smiling as if he had been enjoying himself.

"If you could tell them how never to start you'd be doing something," Roger said, and took out cigarettes. "Have one?"

Richard almost burst with laughter.

"Dad," Scoopy said, "Mum's gone across to Mrs Pearson's. She said she wouldn't be long, and if you were very hungry I was to go and get her."

"I'm ravenous," Roger said. "You two boys go and cook me some sausages and eggs; there's no need to disturb your mother."

Richard was reluctant to go. Scoopy accepted the inevitable more readily, but hesitated in the doorway and asked: "Shall we see you again, sir?"

"If not tonight, another night," Spendlove promised.

"I hope we'll see you often," enthused Richard.

The door closed on them, and Roger lit his own and Spendlove's cigarettes. Spendlove's glass was half full, and Roger poured himself out a whisky and soda, then sat back in an easy chair which was soon to be re-upholstered. The room was to be the last one decorated, and the work was being started upstairs.

"Nice boys you have there," Spendlove remarked. "Fit sons for a hero."

"Don't you start that."

"Damned good show, but it seems to have taken the stuffing out of you," the newspaperman said. "I had my head down for a couple of hours this afternoon; pity you couldn't have done the same. Gibson turned up yet?"

"No."

"Worried?"

"You didn't come here to find out how I'm feeling," Roger said. "What have you come for?"

"You'll probably want to throw me out."

"I do, anyhow."

Spendlove said: "Handsome, you and I have a lot in common. Believe it or not, if I hadn't been a newspaperman I would have wanted to be a detective! One reason I didn't was that I knew my conscience would nag me too much. Like yours. I feel as uneasy as hell."

"Why?"

"In case more babies are on the list."

"Every Division is keeping a special watch on babies, and AS Division extra-specially," Roger said, and drank deeply.

"I knew I needn't have worried, but I did," Spendlove said. "Thanks. Now I'll really stick my neck out. I've had an idea."

"What have I missed?" asked Roger.

"Could Cartwright be being framed? A preparation for blackmail, perhaps?"

Roger didn't answer.

"I know it sounds damned silly," Spendlove said, "but the whole business is peculiar. The more I think of it the less I see Cartwright as a baby-killer, but I think he would have worn down Anne Kindle's resistance sooner or later. From what the neighbours say, she has grounds in plenty for divorce; there wouldn't be any difficulty about one. From all I've heard, Cartwright had no resentment against the child, simply against the fact that it stopped him and her from going out a bit. He would gladly have taken on the child."

"Where did you learn all this?"

"My Territorial Army friends."

"Go on," said Roger, and drained his glass and stood up. Spendlove's glass was empty, and he took it to the small table where the whisky and the soda were.

"Why that particular baby, and why then?" asked Spendlove. "That's what worries me. And there's also the possible connection with the other child who was murdered last week. Then – Cartwright isn't a fool. He may be a bit crazy over this woman, but apart from that he has his head screwed on. Why did he run away?"

"Ledbetter says because he was guilty."

"Ledbetter could be right," agreed Spendlove. "He'd know that by running he was making it look as if he were guilty. If everything else had been all right, I don't think he would have run. I'd like to know what made him."

"Don't you think he committed suicide?"

Spendlove asked sharply: "Found his body?"

"No."

"I was afraid for a moment that you had," the newspaperman said. "No, I don't think he's the suicidal type. I don't believe that he drove the car to the river, either."

"Good job you're not a policeman," Roger said dryly, and handed Spendlove his glass. "We still have to go on the facts."

"Can you prove that he did drive it there?"

"On circumstantial evidence."

Spendlove said: "Handsome, I know I'm probably talking out of the back of my neck, but I wouldn't have come here if I hadn't felt strongly about it. It's the baby angle. I take it you know that Edward Maddison—"

"Has a young wife and a young baby."

Spendlove said: "I wanted to get out to Esher today, but couldn't fit it in."

"General neglect of Mrs Maddison," Roger said dryly. He lifted up the telephone, dialled a Kingston number, and asked for

Superintendent Boon. Spendlove watched intently, as Roger asked questions. Yes, Maddison had reached home before six o'clock. He and his wife were still indoors. Their resident staff, a man and woman, were middle-aged – the man an ex-policeman. The resident nurse was a local girl. Yes, the house would be watched during the night.

Roger was warm in his thanks as he rang off.

"So it's got you like that, too," Spendlove remarked. "I don't like the feel of this job – do you?"

"No."

"I've been dabbling in crime for nearly as long as you, and I've a nose for it," Spendlove said. "I don't think this case is what it seems. There's a nasty stench about. I picked up a rumour that Gibson's officially missing. Is that true?"

"Yes," Roger answered simply.

"Edgy about him?"

"Yes."

"You see what I mean," Spendlove said, almost too intensely. "It isn't running a normal course at all. I know that I'm probably trying to find something which will fit the facts, as I'd like to find them. I'd like to find that Cartwright isn't guilty, and that he is being framed."

"I asked you once, what makes you think that he might be being framed?"

Spendlove hesitated.

"In about five minutes my supper will be ready," Roger said. "Like to share it?"

"No, thanks," Spendlove said, and then gave a rather fierce grin. "What did you make of Edward Maddison?"

"Autocratic throwback spoiled by his staff."

"Ah!"

"Don't be so cryptic."

"The kind who would demand and obtain implicit loyalty and obedience," Spendlove said. "The whole of the Maddison-Cartwright family has been built up like that. I know. I read the history of the firm during that carpet smuggling business a few years back. I did a piece on the romance of carpet making and buying – you probably don't remember. Maddison Brothers is the oldest firm in the country, it exports the finest carpets from the most out-of-the-ordinary places, and it's been built up on the personalities of various heads of the family. There's a kind of tradition: the Boss is really the Boss. Now the Boss is Edward Maddison. I think Cartwright would do whatever his uncle told him to do."

"Even to taking a murder rap?"

"Temporarily."

"Or threatening his baby cousin?"

"That's right – Maddison's child," Spendlove said. "We both see how bad it could be."

"Yes, but don't quote me," Roger said.

"I won't. I can say I got it from somewhere else," Spendlove promised, still looking uneasy. "I don't know what it amounts to, but it's a fact that the future of Maddison Brothers lies with Edward Maddison, his new son, and Roy Cartwright."

"That much even I know," Roger said wryly, "but I can't find an explanation which fits the facts."

"Keep at it," urged Spendlove, in a firmer voice. "I ought to have known that I wouldn't be ahead of you, but there was a chance. Found any reason why Cartwright might have wanted the Shaw child dead?"

"That first murder, you mean?" Roger said. "No, I don't know of a motive. Now tell me why you really came to see me."

"To find out if you were on to the Maddison family and inheritance angle," Spendlove answered. "I'll be off before the smell of those sausages drives me away! Oh, thanks for the tip this afternoon. Anything I can do for you at the moment?"

"Yes," Roger said.

"Name it."

"I've changed my mind. Tell your readers that this is almost certainly a psychopathic job, and play up the fact that Gibson's disappeared."

"Really think it's a psycho job?" asked Spendlove.

"Obviously it could be," Roger answered, "but I'm not talking about schizophrenia, or possible insanity. Psychopaths often have motives, a deep-seated cause to hate, and some shock jolts them into taking action. But I needn't tell you that! Tie everything up, will you, including the fact that Gibson was last seen at Maddison's place, that Cartwright is the junior director of Maddison's, and that the Maddison baby has been threatened."

Spendlove looked eager.

"In other words, make Edward Maddison hopping mad."

"That's right."

"Scare him, too?"

"If he's scarable," Roger said. "A column on his marriage and the new baby wouldn't do any harm at all."

"You really want Aunt Martha on that angle."

"I'll get her, too, if you're not quick about it," Roger said.

"Talk to her anyhow," Spendlove advised. "We want this story spread far and wide. You needn't tell her about the threat!"

Richard came hurrying along the passage to announce that Roger's supper was ready. The smell of sausages was appetising, but there was an odour of burnt toast. Spendlove went off. Roger said: "Keep everything under the grill, Fish, I won't be a minute," and hurried back to the telephone and dialled the *Gazette*. "Give me Aunt Martha," he said when the operator answered, and the name was so general that there was not a moment's hesitation; and Martha Wise was in.

"Roger West here," Roger said. "Could you do some sob-stuff on Mrs Edward Maddison's great interest in young babies and things?"

"I'm doing it now," Aunt Martha told him, sweetly.

Roger was smiling as he went into the kitchen. The boys had excelled themselves; there were four sausages, two eggs, three rashers of bacon and some crisply fried bread. Neither asked, but each was ready with a plate for a second supper. Roger ate ravenously, but said little. The boys, used to such spells of preoccupation, did not worry him with questions. He tried to convince himself that Spendlove had told all he knew, but was by no means certain. He also tried to make some kind of logical sequence of the different factors which the newspaperman had introduced, but could not.

Was Cartwright being framed?

Was there any family feud or jealousy?

Did the new Maddison baby offer any threat to Cartwright's future in the firm?

Cartwright was still missing and so was Gibson; and a psychopathic killer might still be on the prowl. It was a hell of a case.

Hilda Maddison was very young and very lovely, and she had a really beautiful body. She had modelled for one of the great fashion houses for two years before marrying Maddison, and she had learned to carry herself superbly, and to wear and select only those clothes which really suited her. She was usually bright-eyed, alert and, as far as one could tell, thoroughly contented with her lot.

And she loved her child with a passionate love.

She was a paragon of a wife, and did absolutely everything that her husband required of her – provided he told her what to do.

For she had never been able to think for herself. Before Maddison had come along, she had been engaged six or seven times, only for the engagement to be broken off 'by mutual consent'. In fact, she was almost simple. All her reactions were by the book, and her ideas were culled from weekly magazines of the more popular kind. She was sweet, charming, lovely, she had been chaste and virginal, perhaps the most beautiful shell of a woman in London. She had even allowed herself to be trained so that she could talk intelligently for a few minutes, and few of her casual acquaintances suspected the truth of her simplicity.

Anyone who tried to spend half an hour in her company began to suspect the truth: that she had nothing to say in spite of her beautifully modulated voice.

That night, about the time that Roger was eating his supper and Spendlove was driving back to Fleet Street, Hilda was watching television. She was alone in the living-room of the lovely house at Esher. Edward was in his study upstairs, and the married couple who ran the house were at their own television set. Hilda watched the antics of a comedian with the intensity of a child, smiled or laughed with the unseen audience and seemed to have no interest at all except the screen. But quite suddenly, and for no apparent reason, she stood up from a soft couch, and went out, walked straight to the stairs rather as if she believed that she was being watched by a crowd of buyers and prospective customers, went up the wide staircase, which was brightly lit, passed the door of her husband's study without a glance, and went into the small room, next to her bedroom, where the baby slept. This was the nurse's night off.

There was a glow of light near the door, enough to show the outline of the cot and, when she drew nearer, enough to see the outline of a child's head and face. Hilda reached the side of the cot, and then stared down. The television was blaring, and with the door open it sounded very loud, but she took no notice of this, just stared at the child. When the study door opened, she glanced round, but did not move. She heard Edward's footsteps, and he appeared in the doorway, saying: "Hilda, my pet, must you leave the door open so that the television sounds all over the house?"

Hilda didn't answer, but turned to look at him, and he had never seen greater intensity on her face; never seen such emotion as there was now.

"If anything should happen to my baby, I would kill myself," she said. "I mean every word of that."

She had taken the phrase out of a book, Maddison knew, and had uttered it a dozen times today: he also knew that, at the moment she said it, she meant it.

"But nothing will happen to him," Maddison said soothingly. "If you'd be happier, I will arrange for a second nurse, a night nurse—"

"I don't want anyone here I don't know," Hilda answered sharply. "I don't trust anyone, Edward; you know that. Have they caught Roy yet?"

"My dear, I wish you wouldn't talk as if Roy were a hunted criminal. He—"

"I shan't feel safe until he's caught," Hilda declared. "His name wouldn't be in the papers like it is unless the police were pretty sure. If anything happened to my baby, I would kill myself."

Maddison went to her, slipped his arm round her shoulders and together they looked down on the child, until he said: "I think I would too, Hilda. But nothing will happen, you know. The police will take care of that."

"But that man who telephoned meant what he said!"

"There are a lot of cruel, vicious men who enjoy causing pain and anxiety, and I believe the man who spoke to you was one of those. Now come along, precious. Don't worry yourself about things which will never happen."

That was the moment when the telephone bell rang. Hilda jumped wildly, and rushed towards the study, as if determined to make sure that her husband could not get to the telephone first.

As she put the instrument to her ear, a man said: "Make the most of the time you've got left with your baby."

"It was a soft voice, with nothing particular to identify it by," reported the Yard man who was tapping the Maddison's telephone. "The woman gasped, and then Maddison shouted into the telephone, but the caller had rung off. It was a London call, so there's no hope of tracing it."

Chapter Fourteen

Third Victim?

Little Alice Graham was a very different type in every way from Hilda Maddison, although she came from the same background. She was so small and looked so young that many people found it difficult to believe that she was the mother of three children, one of them seven years old, the last a two-month old girl. Alice Graham was a bright, vivacious, hard-working and good-natured woman, her mind as sharp as a needle. Apart from running her home, bringing up the children and looking after her husband – a man crippled two years before by poliomyelitis – she helped to run the small carpentry business which George Graham had operated for years before his disaster. She had kept the business together while he had been away for nearly a year; had kept on the workmen; and, now that he was back and working from his wheelchair, she did all the clerical work, answered the telephone, booked the orders, and generally behaved as a woman-of-all-work.

She was one of the happiest women alive.

That night she was humming to herself while darning the older boy's socks. The radio was on. Television was a dream to come when they were prosperous, because neither parent was prepared to buy anything on the hire-purchase system. All the children were upstairs in the three-bedroomed house on the borders of Acton and Ealing. George was still at the workshop, and would probably not be home until after eleven o'clock; it was now half-past nine.

She had the radio tuned in very low, and every now and again she would get up, go to the door and listen to the silence. After the last trip, she went to the dresser drawer in the small living-room cum kitchen, opened it to get out her sewing box, and saw the silver paper which had been torn when the children had shared half of a large slab of chocolate that afternoon. She hesitated, looking elfin-young, and her eyes were glowing. She put her head on one side, said: "I shouldn't," and then picked up what was left of the slab, broke a small piece off and popped it into her mouth. She gave a comical little grimace, took out the box and slammed the drawer, and went back to her chair. It was a rocking chair with a restricted movement, and she swayed to and fro in it. The radio music stopped, and a man began to talk about education. She listened to this with one ear, hummed to herself and, after ten minutes, got up again and went to the passage door. It was still silent outside.

Coming back, she glanced at the chocolate drawer, shook her head firmly, went to a chair – and then thought that she heard a sound. She stood quite still, looking round at the door. Had it been one of the children she would have known at once, but this was a kind of click, and she felt sure that it had not been from the radio.

It was not often that she felt nervous, but folded on a corner of the table was the *Evening Globe,* carrying the story of the murdered child, and the missing Cartwright; there was also an article connecting the baby murder with one which had taken place last week. She moved very quickly towards the door, a little tense and pale, gripped the handle, and pulled.

It did not open.

Alice Graham turned it again, and the handle moved freely enough. She pulled again. The door had stuck; but she had never known it happen before, George always made sure that everything worked smoothly and well. She tried again, shaking the door, but it held fast.

Suddenly, she cried: "Oh, God, no!"

She darted across the room towards the telephone, and snatched up the receiver, then dialled 999. In spite of a surge of frenzy, she did it all very deliberately. Her heart was pounding, and she could hardly hear the voice of the operator, who asked almost disinterestedly: "What service do you want, please?"

"Police." Alice made herself say carefully. "This is Acton 01523. Someone is trying to kidnap my baby."

"Will you please—"

Alice put the receiver down quickly. It seemed an age before she moved, but she tried the door handle, with the same result: and then she threw back her head and screamed.

There must be someone up there; she felt sure that it was the baby-killer, but it was not only panic which made her scream; she wanted to frighten anyone who was up there.

She heard footsteps above her head, and thought she heard a cry. In one swift movement she reached the radio and switched it off, and then screamed again. Her heart was pounding, and she felt an awful fear, but she knew that she had to *do* something. She went to the window overlooking the back garden, and her fingers trembled as she unfastened the latch. She was trembling all over when she flung up the window. She saw the light at her neighbour's window opposite, but they had the television, and it was usually on loud.

She climbed through the window, and as she stepped on to the path leading from the street to the garden, she heard, a man shout: "What's the matter?"

"Help!" Alice shouted. "My baby! *Help, help!*"

She heard heavy footsteps not far away. There was light at the street, and as she raced towards it, she saw a policeman swinging towards the little gate, only twenty yards away from her.

"There's a man upstairs. He locked me in!" she cried, and did not know how to speak coherently. "There's a man—"

"Got the front door key?" the policeman snapped.

She had forgotten that; she had been so cool and determined, but she had forgotten that vital thing. She turned on her heel, but the policeman said: "Get to a telephone and dial 999."

"I have, I—"

"All right," the policeman said firmly. "I'll stop him. Probably just a burglar." He swung towards the front door ;and she saw him bend his elbow as he reached the front room window. Glass crashed. He seemed not to worry about splinters, but put his shoulder forward and climbed through. A man on the other side of the road called out: "Anything the matter?" Alice saw the policeman climbing, and went after him blindly. The street lamp showed just enough light for the man, and she knew that he would be able to see the door.

Then, the front door opened. She screamed: "There he is!"

She saw a man appear in the doorway. He wore a long coat and a cap pulled down over his face, and she could see only his shape and the glint of his eyes. She was only a few yards away from him, and she felt paralysed. The man on the other side of the road called again: "Anything the matter?"

Alice flung herself at the man who was rushing from her house, but as she reached him he kicked out, and she felt the sharpness of his toecap on her knee. She cried out, staggered and fell. She saw the man dart to one side. She saw the policeman appear, without his helmet. She tried to get up, and so hampered the policeman, while the intruder was racing along the street, and the man in the road was shouting:

"Stop thief! Police!"

Alice said in a choking whisper: "Oh, God, not my baby," as she struggled to her feet.

Police Constable Stevens of the local Division, who had been patrolling the street when he had heard this woman screaming, now saw the man racing towards the end of the street, heard the man shouting, and heard this woman saying in a terrified voice: "Oh, God, not my baby." All the horror one could imagine was in her voice and her expression as she fought to get to her feet. Then a car's headlights swept the street, and Stevens knew that a Flying Squad car had arrived. Its occupants would almost certainly see the running man. He shouted across to the man on the other side of the road: "Tell them which way he went!"

Then he turned to follow the woman into the house. She was limping, and put out a hand to support herself. He could tell the terror she felt, the dread she had of what she might find. She tried to hurry, but could not.

Stevens said sharply: "Let me go first."

He took his torch from a hook inside his tunic, flashed it on, and shone it on the stairs. They were covered with a patterned carpet. He pushed past the woman, who was still limping, and found the light switch. As the light came on, he told himself that his first job was to find out what had happened. He started up the stairs, and thought he heard a whimper of sound, but he knew that there were three children in this household. He tried to tell himself that there was not the slightest reason to believe that this had been a visit from a baby-killer. He failed to convince himself. He reached the landing, and had to call: "Which room?"

He heard the mother say: "Straight—straight ahead." She was halfway up the stairs, and standing still for a moment; obviously her knee hurt badly. He went straight into the room in front of him. The door was wide open, and no light was on. He pressed the switch by the door, but nothing happened. He tried to keep the beam of his own torch steady as he flashed it. The beam fell on a cot; as he stepped further into the room he saw that it was against the wall on the right, safely out of the draught from door and window.

He saw the child.

Asleep? Or dead? He went closer, gritting his teeth, and the light fell on its eyes, and its eyes opened. He swung round.

"She's alive!" he cried. "It's all right!" Then he went down on one knee, and picked the child up.

Roger heard the telephone in the middle of a boxing programme. The boys were intent on the screen, and Janet was ironing on the other side of the living-room at the back of the house. He got up, and went into the hall, where there was an extension, of the telephone. He felt edgy; he had been all night, especially since he had been told about the telephone call to Maddison's house. He sensed that Janet was looking at him but was forcing herself not to complain; he had seen how white she had been when she had read of the incident on the turntable. He winked at her, and lifted the telephone, leaving the door open. The boys turned down the volume of the television. "Roger West here."

"Sorry to worry you, Mr West." So it was the Yard again. "But there has been another baby incident, at Acton. The child doesn't seem to have been hurt, but the attacker got away. Mr. Hennessy asked you to go right away. The address is—"

"I'm on my way," Roger said, a moment later.

It was almost a relief to go out on a job, not to have to 'rest' while wondering what was happening outside, wondering where Gibson was; wondering.

Chapter Fifteen

Hunt

Roger saw the little woman in the front room of the narrow terraced house, and thought that she looked tired but radiant. She was so tiny that she hardly came up to the shoulders of massive Superintendent Hennessy of the BS Division, who was in the room with her. Roger stepped into an ordinary front room in an ordinary suburban three-bed-roomed house. The baby lay asleep in an armchair, with another chair pushed up close, to make sure that it could not wriggle out.

"Everything all right, Mrs Graham?" Roger asked.

"This is Superintendent West, of New Scotland Yard," Hennessy introduced.

"Yes, everything's wonderful now, and my husband will soon be home," answered Mrs Graham. "I don't know what would have happened without that policeman, though."

"One of our chaps was in the street," Hennessy explained.

"He was wonderful!"

Roger said dryly: "Aren't all policemen supposed to be?"

Mrs Graham laughed excitedly, then turned to look down at her child, and obviously forgot Roger. Hennessy went out with Roger, and they seemed to fill the little staircase.

"Thank God it wasn't worse," Hennessy said. "No doubt the swine was going to kill the kid."

"Positive?"

"Come and see for yourself."

In the tiny bedroom where the cot was, three policemen were working – one taking photographs, two searching the floor and the cot, which had already been tested for fingerprints; a black powder had been used on the pale-blue paint. On a double bed, spread out on a large sheet of brown paper, were several things from the cot, including the pillow.

"Just the same as with the other baby jobs," Hennessy said. "The pillow was on one side. Obviously it had been held over the baby's mouth – there are slight sick marks dead centre of the pillow."

Roger nodded.

"If the child had just dribbled, the marks would have been one side or the other," Hennessy said, hammering his point home. "Anyhow, the baby was lying on the mattress and the pillow was at the side. The baby couldn't have moved it."

"Speaks for itself," Roger agreed. "We had any luck?"

"Any luck, Smith?" Hennessy asked one of the men.

"Could be a couple of footprints," reported Smith. He was tall, dark and very thin, and his eyes had a baleful look. He indicated two circles chalked on the linoleum, and lying across the lines were two pieces of cardboard, to make sure that nothing could destroy marks beneath them. "No fingerprints, though. He wore gloves."

"Hm. How long will it be before we can see photographs of those footprints?"

"First thing in the morning, sir."

"Can't we get a better light?" Roger asked, and looked up at a low wattage bulb.

"The intruder broke one, and this is the only one we could get. I've sent for more," Hennessy said. "Use your torch, Smith."

Smith went down on one knee, and removed the cardboard as if it were both fragile and precious. Then he shone a torch on to the polished linoleum.

Roger saw at once what had happened. When this floor had been polished, two small patches had been missed with the actual polishing, so that there had been a slight smear of wax polish. The intruder had stepped on these. The shiny floor had taken no impression of his feet, but the dull patches showed a heel, and one showed a heel and toe. Only a very quick and smart officer would have seen those; and the luck had been with them, for no one else had smeared the prints.

"Damned smart," Roger said, and Smith stopped looking baleful. "See I get plenty of prints, too, and telephone a description to the Yard. What size boots, would you think?"

"Eight and a half or nine."

"Cartwright wears a nine," declared Hennessy.

"Yes," Roger said. "Thanks, Smith." He led the way downstairs, and Hennessy was smiling as if at some secret joke. "Where's this copper who came to the rescue?"

"Out on the beat," answered Hennessy. "I don't believe in spoiling my chaps. He should be along in five minutes or so. I'll have him brought in." He led the way into a small kitchen. "The woman really did the job; she dialled 999 and then kicked up a hell of a row. Scared the swine off."

"She see him?"

"Just the figure of a man, cap pulled over his face. She says medium size."

"Any other witness?"

"Man across the road didn't come near enough to see the attacker, but says he was wearing a dark coat, and then he dropped his cap at the end of the street, but that was too far away to get a clear sight of him. He's not sure of the man's size, says the coat seemed to billow out and make him look big."

"One of our chaps on the spot and a Squad car on the way – how did the chap get away?" Roger demanded.

"Had a motor-cycle waiting," Hennessy said. "I've a couple of chaps looking at the spot where it was parked; we might get something from the tyre marks. By the time the Squad car was on the spot, he'd got too far away. I put out a call for all motor-cycles to be stopped – don't know whether there's been any luck."

"We'd have heard if there had been," Roger said. "Our best chance is that footprint."

"One thing's certain: only a psycho would keep doing this," Hennessy declared. "Whether it's Cartwright or not I don't know. Cartwright got any reason to hate babies?"

"I'm trying to find out," Roger said. "I'm going to have another word with Mrs Graham." He went into the other room, where the young mother was still excited, and asked, as if casually: "Do you know Maddison, the carpet people, Mrs Graham?"

"Oh yes," said the woman promptly. "I worked there until I was married.

So it was beginning to add up, Roger thought grimly, and stood studying the woman while other possibilities flashed through his mind. There were a dozen things he wanted to check urgently, among them whether Mrs Shaw as well as Mrs Kindle had worked at Maddisons. Mrs Graham was looking at him intently, as if puzzled by his manner, and he asked quickly: "How long were you with the firm?"

"Just over ten years. I went there straight from school."

"Did you know Mr Cartwright?" Roger was ready for the slightest sign that the question worried the woman.

"Well, not really," she answered. "He was a schoolboy most of my time – he first came into the firm a few months before I left." She could not have been more untroubled.

"Did you know Mr Maddison?"

"Of course – everyone did."

"Did you know Helen Osborn?"

"Oh, yes," said Mrs Graham. "I was in the general office and she was really Mr Maddison's secretary, but Helen and I got along very well. I—"

She stopped abruptly, and the change in her expression was startling; in a moment, she looked both horrified and alarmed.

"What's the matter?" demanded Roger. "You must be absolutely frank with me."

"Yes," she promised huskily. "There's no reason why I shouldn't. I—I just realised that Anne Blythe, Anne Kindle as she is now, worked at Maddisons too, and her baby—" She broke off.

Roger said quietly: "Do you know Mrs Shaw?"

"Shaw?"

"A Mrs Shaw lost her baby in the same way last week," Roger reminded her.

"Oh," said Mrs Graham, heavily. "I—I don't know her, I as far as I'm aware, but then, Shaw's her married name, isn't it? I thought she was rather like a girl in the salesrooms, Joyce Barber, but—"

Mrs Shaw's Christian name was Joyce, Roger knew.

Here was a new angle that might lead to the answer: three young mothers, all employed at one time by Maddisons, all victims of the baby-killer, all acquainted with Edward Maddison and with others at the Maddison warehouse and offices; all in some way associated with Roy Cartwright, too.

Now Mrs Graham had a scared look.

Roger said. "Mrs Graham, I want you to think of anyone – any man – known to all three of you: Joyce Barber or Shaw, Anne Blythe or Kindle, and yourself – anyone who might have a reason to want to make all of you suffer. Anyone who—"

"You mean, anyone who was in love with us, or thought he was," said Mrs Graham quietly. "I wouldn't know about the others, but there were only two men who ever took any notice of me. One's married and went to Australia, and the other one—" She hesitated, and then went on very quietly: "I don't know that I ought to name anyone, Mr West."

"Unless he's mixed up in these crimes, he'll never know," Roger assured her. "Who was it, please?"

"Mr Maddison," answered Mrs Graham flatly. "He said he was in love with me, but I never took him seriously."

Perhaps that had been her great mistake.

"Say nothing of these questions to anyone, please," Roger warned. "And you won't be involved unless it's vital." He wished her good-night, and went out, impressed by her intent and worried look, and positive about one thing: she had hated naming Maddison.

It was a little after ten o'clock when Roger went outside and found a spit of rain in the air. A policeman was approaching smartly, and Hennessy came up and said: "Here's the man who was on the spot, Superintendent."

Roger saw a surprisingly young face beneath a surprisingly large helmet. "Nice work," he said, "keep it up."

"Thank you, sir!"

"All right, Stevens," Hennessy said, and Stevens went on less smartly, but obviously glowing, to pound his beat. Roger went to his car. "Some people are lucky," Hennessy grumbled. "It will be hours before I can get to bed."

"If I'm wanted urgently," Roger said, "try Edward Maddison's house, 17 The Close, Esher."

Hennessy had the grace to grin.

Roger drove to the corner, turned it, and then radioed the Yard. He had not wanted Hennessy to know of the latest development yet; the Divisional man might not be able to resist questioning Mrs Graham, and it would be wiser not to question her too deeply yet.

"Is Mr Evans still on duty?" Roger asked the Yard.

"Yes, sir, I'll put you through," and Roger waited only a moment before Evans came on.

"Yes, sir?"

"Here's a new line," Roger said at once. "Check whether Mrs Shaw was a Joyce Barber before she was married, and also check if she worked at Maddisons. We know already that Mrs Kindle worked there."

"Gawd!" exclaimed Evans.

"If they did work at Maddisons, find out if anyone there ever set their caps at them."

"Such as who?"

"Anyone."

"Right!" Evans exclaimed.

Roger drove on, heading for Brentford and Kew Bridge.

He knew this side of London thoroughly, and knew every short cut to Kingston and then out to Esher. It would be more than half-past ten when he arrived, but he had no doubt at all that he should go and try to shake Maddison.

Had Maddison or had Cartwright any cause for hating the babies of these three women? Had there been anything in their lives which might have turned their minds against them? Had Cartwright, for instance, received any recent shock which might affect him?

It was twenty minutes to eleven when Roger stopped outside number 17, The Close. There was a street lamp outside, and a light at the front door of the house itself. He knew the district and the type of house well, and was quite sure that this came into the luxury class. He waited at the gate for a moment, and heard a rustle of movement, glanced round, and saw a man standing just inside the garden.

"I'm Superintendent West," Roger said.

"That's a relief," the man said, as if he really meant it. "Good-evening, sir."

"Everything quiet?"

"Yes, sir."

"Have we got a chap at the back?"

"Two."

"Thanks. What can you tell me about Maddison?"

"Not really a lot. This isn't my usual district," the man said. "There are the two living-in servants, ex-Constable Mayhew and wife, and there's a nursemaid who's still out. Maddison's in, and so is his wife. I don't know about baby-killing, but this was a case of baby-snatching all right!"

"Like that, is it? I'm told she's a beauty."

"But dumb," the policeman said.

Roger smiled as he walked up to the front porch. It was always a reassuring thing to find the police on top of their job, and obviously nothing would be allowed to slip up here. The telephone calls did their damage psychologically by striking fear. The baby might be in some kind of danger, and Cartwright might try to get in touch with his uncle, so there were the two reasons for keeping the house under close surveillance.

As Roger reached the porch, the light went out. He could not find the bell push, and waited for a moment. He heard footsteps, and judged that two people were going upstairs. He waited until they were probably halfway up, and then rang the bell. He heard an exclamation, and stood back from the porch. After a moment, the light went on again, dazzling. The door opened, and Maddison appeared. Behind him, on a wide flight of stairs, was one of the most beautiful young women imaginable; beautiful enough to catch Roger's eye, although his main interest was in Maddison.

"Who—" Maddison began, and then obviously saw who it was; annoyance sharpened in his voice. "I really must protest at this intrusion, sir."

"I want to see you urgently," Roger said. He stepped forward so that Maddison was forced to give way a little. He could see the man's grey eyes, the way he frowned, the fact that he did not like this kind of treatment. The woman had a scared look. She was wearing a silken housecoat, high at the neck, shaped to her figure; the I-want-to-look-as-if-I've-been-poured-into-it kind. He judged that she was in the early twenties. "Good-evening, Mrs Maddison," he said. "Have you seen Mr Cartwright this evening?"

"What on earth—" Maddison began, only to stop as if he realised that he wasn't doing very well.

His wife answered: "No, I haven't." Now there was no doubt of the alarm which showed in her blue eyes. "He hasn't come here, has he? He's not—" She broke off, as her voice rose to screaming point.

"If my nephew had been here I would have informed the police immediately," Maddison said coldly. "Hilda, I should go upstairs. I will deal with Mr West." He sounded rather like a headmaster knowing that he had a tough customer to handle. "I won't be long."

"Have you seen Mr Cartwright this week?" Roger asked the wife.

"No!" she exclaimed. "I—" She moved suddenly, coming down the stairs, and demanded tensely: "Why haven't you found him? Why are you letting him run loose? Don't you know that he's—"

"*Hilda!*" rapped Maddison.

She flashed those beautiful blue eyes on him. She was much closer to Roger now, her lips were parted, her hands were clenched, and for a moment it looked as if she were going to allow Maddison to make her keep quiet. But in a high-pitched voice she went on: "I won't be silenced like a little girl. Roy is ever so dangerous. You know as well as I do. It's a wicked thing that the police haven't caught him."

Roger said swiftly: "We can't catch him while his friends and relations are protecting him, Mrs Maddison."

"West, if you—" Maddison began savagely.

"Edward! Is that true?" Hilda Maddison swung round on her husband, and rushed at him in such a way that it looked as if she would strike him. "Are you hiding Roy? If you are, I'll never forgive you."

"Hilda, this man is deliberately trying to upset you," Maddison asserted, and he gave a sharp impression that he was fighting for composure. "I would like you to go upstairs, and I will join you in a very few minutes."

"I won't go until I know whether you're hiding Roy!"

Maddison looked at her very straightly, and said: "No, my dear. I am not hiding Roy. I have not seen or heard from him since the day before yesterday. This man is trying to make you believe circumstances which are not true. Now, please, go upstairs."

She looked like a little girl, except that her figure was not that of a girl. When she turned it was with a kind of considered seductiveness, as if she could not resist flaunting her body. Slowly, she went upstairs. Maddison waited until she had disappeared, and then turned to Roger. He was really a strikingly handsome man, and the glitter in his eyes and the set of his jaw gave him more than arrogance; it gave him a look of power.

"I shall report your disgraceful behaviour to the Home Secretary first thing in the morning," he said icily. "Now, if you have any legitimate business with me, send for an assistant. I do not intend to answer any questions without a witness. You have men outside, watching. You are creating the impression that there are reasons to suspect me of complicity in some crime. It is tantamount to defamation of character, and I warn you that—"

"Don't talk like a bloody fool," Roger said roughly. "I'm not having the house watched because you might be hiding Cartwright. I'm having it watched because Cartwright or someone else might come and choke the life out of your son. Mr Maddison, you once showed interest in one of your employees, now a Mrs Anne Graham. Have you seen her since she was married?"

"What the devil do you mean, sir?"

"I'm asking a simple question."

Maddison hesitated for what seemed a long time, and then answered: "I have not."

"Have you seen Mrs Shaw, a Miss Joyce Barber before she was married, in recent months?" That was a long shot.

This time there was a shorter pause, and Maddison answered more quietly: "No. What makes you ask these questions?"

"Mr Maddison, I am a police officer carrying out his duty, and in the course of it I come across a great deal of information. I never divulge the source of it unless it is necessary to in the interests of justice. I have reason to believe that from time to time you have made advances to certain young women on the staff of Maddisons, including Miss Barber, Miss Blythe, now Mrs Kindle—"

"Are you trying to suggest that I have been associated with the mothers of these dead babies?" Maddison demanded, and he went pale.

Roger simply nodded.

He heard a faint sound at a door upstairs, and guessed that Maddison's wife was at it. He could not be sure whether she had heard her husband, whose voice was very low-pitched. Maddison seemed oblivious of everything except Roger, as he went on: "Yes, I was interested in these girls. That is no crime, I know nothing whatever about the murder of these children. I don't believe my nephew does, either."

Then the door opened and Maddison's wife came downstairs.

Chapter Sixteen

Cause for Hate?

The intrusion was exactly what Roger wanted. The woman would be far easier to question than Maddison, and now there would be no keeping her out of the picture. Many people would blame him for playing on a mother's fears, but Ledbetter would approve; and there was far more at stake than this one woman's peace of mind.

Maddison said in a low-pitched voice, close to Roger's ear: "If you don't put her mind at rest about my nephew, I'll—"

"Stop whispering!" Hilda called as she reached the hall. Her cheeks were flushed and her eyes sparkling with anger. "I want to know the truth. I don't care about these other women – you didn't marry them – but I don't believe that you've been telling me the truth about Roy. I believe you know that Roy's gone mad. Did *you* know?" She spun round towards Roger. "Did you know that Roy tried to stop our marriage? Did you know that *my* son will inherit everything he thought *he* was going to inherit? Go on, tell me. Did you know how he hated me and my child? *Did you know?*"

Now was the opportunity to get Maddison on his side, if he were innocent; and if he were involved in the murders, no harm would come now by pretending to believe what he had said.

Roger said, very quietly: "Mr Maddison has told us enough to warn us, Mrs Maddison."

Hilda looked astonished. "He *has?*"

Maddison moistened his lips, gulped, and for the first time looked really ill.

Roger said easily: "In a case of divided loyalties, it isn't always easy to do the wise thing, but Mr Maddison succeeded." That kind of corny statement would impress this woman, and he saw the sudden delight with which she smiled at Maddison. Then with almost embarrassing abandon she flung herself at her husband, pressed her lovely body against his, kissed him on the mouth, and cried: "Oh, Teddy, you darling!"

A minute later, she waved from the top of the stairs. In that moment she reminded Roger of little Mrs Graham; she had the same kind of radiance. Now he glanced about him, at the luxury of panelled walls, thick carpets, beautiful pictures, and he contrasted it with the frugal simplicity of Alice Graham's home.

Maddison said: "Come this way, please," and led the way into a drawing-room of green and gold, beautifully furnished in eighteenth century French style, the kind of room in which Janet would hesitate to sit down, in case she spoiled something. Maddison went to a magnificent cabinet which had panelled paintings on the front, opened it, and revealed an array of bottles and glasses. "What will you have, Mr West?"

"Whisky and soda, please," Roger said.

Maddison poured out two; his own perhaps a little stronger than Roger's. He handed one to Roger, said: "To your success," and drank deeply. He was pale, and obviously badly shaken by both disclosures. He moistened his lips and looked steadily enough into Roger's eyes. Whatever he wanted to say was proving difficult to utter. "I don't know your motives, but I'm grateful for the reassurance that you gave my wife," he said at last. "Thank you."

Roger sipped, then said briskly: "All I want is a child murderer. I don't want to cause domestic trouble here or anywhere else. How long has your nephew resented your marriage?"

"From the time it was first mooted, three years ago."

"Is it true that your infant son will inherit a great deal that would otherwise have gone to Mr Cartwright?"

"Yes."

"How seriously will that affect Mr Cartwright's future?"

"He is never likely to become chairman and certainly will never be chief shareholder of the company."

"Did he show especial resentment after your son was born?"

"Yes."

"Did he threaten the child?"

"Not to my knowledge," Maddison answered, "but he was heard on several occasions to say that he wished the child had never been born."

"Who heard him?" Roger demanded.

"My wife and I, on at least two occasions," Maddison answered, "and he once said the same thing in the hearing of my general manager."

"Ramsbottom?"

"Yes."

Roger made a mental note to check that with the manager, as he went on: "Do you know where your nephew is now?"

"No."

"How did he get out of the warehouse?"

"I understand that he hid among carpets in a van leaving for deliveries to the docks."

"Who told you?"

Maddison wiped the sweat off his forehead.

"The dispatch foreman, a man named Corrissey."

"Did he help your nephew to escape?"

"Yes," answered Maddison, and now he seemed to be on the point of collapse. "Mr West, Corrissey has been in my employ for nearly thirty years. He began here as a boy. He is a hunchback, as you may know, and consequently has certain disabilities, and but for his work here he might have had a very difficult life. He was very grateful, and devoted to the family. When my nephew went to the warehouse and asked for sanctuary, Corrissey gave it to him out of his deep loyalty. He assumed I would wish it, but did not tell me until afterwards. Apparently Roy spent most of the night in one of the vans, and was admitted to the warehouse when Corrissey opened it first thing in the morning. Corrissey gave him food, too."

Maddison dropped into a chair, and wiped his forehead again.

"Why did he leave?" Roger asked sharply.

"Corrissey told me that he had been cooped up in a small storeroom most of the day, because people were always coming in and out, left it to stretch his legs, and was seen by one of your men."

Roger felt his heart thumping; this was as near as he had yet got to word of Gibson.

"What happened then?" he asked.

"Corrissey says that he tripped your man up and rolled him in a carpet to give Roy time to escape. Then Corrrissey"—Maddison gulped—"then he panicked. He realised that he had committed a criminal offence, and he sent your man out – still rolled in a carpet – to the docks. When I heard this I told Corrissey to release him immediately, but Corrissey says that he had already escaped. I am well aware that I should have reported him at once, Mr West, but it seemed cruel to punish a man for his loyalty – and – well, I did nothing."

Roger stared at him coldly, and said: "Which docks?"

"The East London."

"May I use your telephone?"

"Of course, of course."

Roger lifted the receiver, dialled the Yard, and gave orders for the East London docks to be watched, and for Corrissey to be picked up. He replaced the receiver, and said in a flat voice: "That kind of loyalty can get you into serious trouble. Now that we're alone – were these girl employees of yours your mistresses?"

"No!" Maddison exclaimed.

"None of them?"

Maddison said stubbornly: "I don't have to answer personal questions of that nature. I know nothing of the murders. That is all that matters."

"You think your nephew does?"

"You are putting words into my mouth," Maddison protested. "I cannot believe Roy—"

"If he's innocent, why did he run away?"

"I have no idea," said Maddison.

"Who do you think is threatening your own son?"

"I have no idea about that either."

"Do you feel the slightest danger for your own son?"

"Of course I do," Maddison replied sharply. "But I have perfectly capable and trustworthy servants and now that your men are watching there should be no need to worry unduly. Unfortunately my wife is very emotional, and she knows how Roy feels. They have never got on well together. She is passionately devoted to our child, and I find her panic quite understandable."

"Hasn't she greater reason for fear than you've told me?"

"I don't think so. These telephone calls are hellish; but brutes who get a kick out of making others suffer do exist."

"Yes," agreed Roger, and added sharply: "But this man wants you and your wife to suffer, not just anyone. Have you any enemies?"

"I know of none."

"Has Mr Cartwright?"

"I believe that the husband of Mrs Kindle has grounds for disliking him, but I've heard of no one else."

"Have you any reason to believe any other person has cause to hate your wife or you?"

"None whatsoever."

"Have you ever given these young women cause to hate you?"

"No!"

"Did you put any of them with child?" Roger demanded, and was ready to withdraw that question if Maddison protested. But the other man seemed beyond anger.

"No, I did not," he said hoarsely. "There was an association between Miss Helen Osborn and myself, but it ended before my marriage." He was very pale.

"Have you any idea where Miss Osborn is?" Roger demanded.

"She took my man round, didn't she?"

"Yes, she did," answered Maddison. "I haven't seen her since. I assume that she felt the same sense of loyalty as Corrissey, and preferred not to be questioned. I can tell you nothing more, Mr West; nothing at all."

Roger decided not to try to squeeze more out of the man; he could think over all he had said, and come back soon, primed with considered questions. He said good-night, and went out.

The man watching in the garden moved forward as Roger came along the path. The rain had stopped and the moon was up, so that the garden and the nearby house showed vaguely. A long way off a car passed at speed, and in the distance there were the red and green lights of a high-flying aircraft.

"Everything all right, sir?"

"I think so. I shouldn't be too surprised if Cartwright turns up."

"I've a walkie-talkie radio here, sir, and if there's any cause for anxiety I'll call the station."

"Fine," said Roger.

He got into the car, but did not drive away immediately. He switched on the radio, and checked with the Yard. The cap left behind by the assailant of Alice Graham's baby had not been identified, but short, dark hair and tiny pieces of dandruff had been taken from it. The footprint carried no helpful mark. There was no news from the docks or of Corrissey.

"Are you getting the cap size checked?" asked Roger.

"It's seven and a quarter, sir. Cartwright's head size." And Cartwright had dark hair.

"Is there any report of a scuffle near the spot where the cap was found?"

"No, sir."

It was a narrow-peaked cloth cap. There was no wind tonight, and it was difficult to think how it could have been dislodged except in a scuffle – or deliberately. If it were Cartwright's, could it have been thrown down, to point at him?

"Anything else?"

"The man May, who works with Corrissey, swears he didn't see anything. He knows about Cartwright, but says that Corrissey sent him out when Cartwright was in the dispatch room."

"Where is May now?"

"At the Division, sir."

"Tell them I'm going to talk to him," Roger said.

Bert May looked tired to a point of exhaustion and more cretinous than ever, but there was nothing wrong with him, as far as Roger could judge, except that he had been dominated by Corrissey. He swore that he had not seen Gibson or the Osborn girl at all, and had no idea where they had gone. Corrissey, he said, had sent him on an errand, and there was no sign of trouble when he had returned.

"Better let him go," Roger said. "Watch every move he makes, in case Corrissey tries to get at him."

"Tell you one thing," the Divisional man said. "Gibby, Cartwright, and this Osborn girl have all vanished. Must be a junk-hole somewhere."

Roger grunted.

It was after midnight when he reached home. All the lights were out. He left the car outside the garage, in case he needed it in a hurry, and went in. He was used to moving about quietly so as not to disturb Janet; nothing would disturb the boys. He stifled a yawn as he went to the kitchen. There were some sandwiches, but he did not feel hungry, just nibbled at one, and left the others under the dish. He kept yawning as he went upstairs. Janet did not stir when he went into the bedroom, and for once he was sorry; he would have liked to talk. He undressed in the light of a street lamp and the moon, and got into bed. He stretched out, with the warmth of Janet's body by him, and told himself that this was going to be one of the few nights when he could not get off to sleep. It was not only the baby-killer, it was Gibson. And that girl. And the fact that all the bereaved mothers had worked for Maddisons.

"God!" he exclaimed and sprang out of bed, oblivious of Janet, who started up. He ran downstairs to the telephone, yanked the receiver off, and as soon as he was on to the Yard he said: "Urgent job to get started tonight, even if it means dragging people out of bed. We've got to find out if there are any more ex-Maddison employees with young children. The manager, Ramsbottom, is most likely to give information. Don't let him or anyone else put you off. We want details of girls who left to get married, and ..."

It was ten minutes before he went back to bed, had a reassuring word with Janet, and dropped off to sleep.

It was half-past six next morning when a Dutch seaman, emptying a bucket of swill over the side of a freighter registered at Amsterdam, saw the body floating in the water. He knew what it was at once, and stared for a few moments in a kind of awed fascination. Then he rushed to wake the Master. Within two minutes, the River Police had been informed, and a launch arrived alongside the Dutch vessel. The body had floated into a small backwater, which was littered with refuse – cabbage, orange peel, apple cores, paper, everything likely to be thrown overboard from the ships which used London's river.

Using a boathook, one of three policemen pulled the body towards the side of the small boat. It was heavy, and floating face downwards. When it was drawn alongside, another man leaned over and, expertly, the body was brought into the boat. The crew of the Dutch vessel, three dockers, and a small boy were fascinated spectators of all this, and there was a sigh from them all when the body actually flopped into the bottom of the police launch.

The policemen recognised Gibson.

Roger was told the moment he reached the Yard, just after nine o'clock. He went straight upstairs to the laboratory, where Timms, the pathologist on duty, had a report on his desk. The autopsy would be carried out later in the day, but Gibson's clothes were here, and had already been examined.

"The one thing that's certain is that there were some carpet hairs on them," the pathologist said. "I would say they were from an Indian carpet but I couldn't swear to it. Look." He pointed out a number of long, hairy threads which lay on a sheet of white plastic. "One red, one brown, one blue, one green – a multi-coloured carpet all right. There are hairs like these in the turn-ups of the trousers, in the pockets, and down the neck, as if he had been rolled up in a carpet. There were more in the shoes than anywhere else, too. I'd say that he was rolled up in a carpet, that he suffocated to death, and then his body dropped into the river. As soon as the autopsy's done, I'll confirm all that."

There was nothing to do but wait, and plenty to keep Roger busy. He studied all reports on Maddison, Cartwright, Hilda Maddison, Helen Osborn and the bereaved mothers. All of these young women had been approached by Maddison, but another report said that several others had, too.

"Bit of a snag," Evans remarked sourly. "Looks like it. We want to find anyone else who knew them all."

"Lots of people at Maddisons."

"Don't be bloody awkward," Roger said irritably. "I mean who fancied them all. Seen anything about other young ex-Maddison mothers?"

"No – it'll take a long time to find out where they've all gone. Some are in London, but there are others all over the country. I put two men on to it as soon as I came in, and Ramsbottom was here half the night with Maddison's staff records."

"Good enough," Roger said. "What beats me is, where've those others gone?"

"That Osborn girl will turn up in the river, Cartwright too, I wouldn't wonder," Evans prophesied glumly.

He went off, and Roger studied more reports.

Helen Osborn had been Edward Maddison's mistress for several years, and the association had been broken off three years ago. The girl was believed to have been given a down payment as consolation, and a cushy job for life.

Maddison had met his wife at a fashion show where his carpets had been part of the decor; the fact that within a few months they had been married suggested that Hilda had not been so complaisant as Helen Osborn.

Cartwright seemed to have led an ordinary, uneventful life.

At half-past eleven the autopsy report came in, with its grim tidings. Gibson had undoubtedly died from suffocation, and carpet dust – now identified as Mirzapore – was found in his lungs and nose. Once this was known, Roger was quick to sense the mood of everyone at the Yard. Yesterday they had been uneasy, because

Gibson was missing; today, each man felt that it was his responsibility to help to find the murderers. Every Division was alerted, the River Police were checking the most likely places for the body to have been put into the water, and river know-alls came to the conclusion that it had been somewhere on the south side of the river, probably opposite the Tower of London.

"And within half a mile of the Maddison dockside warehouse," Roger said, when he was told. He felt savage with the situation and angry with himself. He also had an oddly guilty and yet relieved feeling. He had sent Gibson to Maddisons – but Gibson had virtually asked to be sent. If he, Roger, had had his own way, he would have gone there, and his body might now have been lying on the mortuary slab.

He was alone in his office when a telephone bell jarred out, and he picked up the receiver with a half fear that this would be more bad news. It was the laboratory chief.

"Bit more for you, Handsome. We've been able to compare the hair and dandruff found in that cap from last night's baby case, and Cartwright's."

"Well?" Roger barked.

"The same," the other assured him.

Now the pointers were really aimed at Cartwright. Given a little more, there would be a tight case against him. Was it too far-fetched to think that the man might have been framed? Was all the evidence too perfect?

Roger was trying to convince himself that it wasn't when the telephone bell rang again.

"West," he said sharply.

"We've cornered Joe Corrissey at Waterloo," a man told him. "Coming?"

Chapter Seventeen

Capture

Roger pulled up at the foot of the steps beneath the great clock at Waterloo station, and jumped out of his car and ran up the steps. Two or three people on the platform stared. He saw a uniformed policeman standing by the nearer bookstall, and made a beeline for the man, who recognised him at once.

"The wanted man's on the line, sir, other end of the platform."

"Right." Roger ran along the wide approach to the platforms. Comparatively few people were about, for the rush hour was over. Music was being relayed over a loudspeaker. A small child got in his way, and he stumbled while avoiding it. He saw the little cinema at the far end of the station, and just beneath it was a cordon of men; obviously these were Divisional and Railway police. He recognised a very fat, flabby man, Largetson, of the local Division, and Largetson beckoned.

Roger reached the cordon.

"Know where he is?" he asked.

"We think he's somewhere under that train," Largetson answered. A long train was standing at the end platform. Its carriages had been freshly washed, and it was streaming with water. A whistle went off, a high-pitched, painful screech of sound. Along the platform policemen in uniform, porters and plain-clothes men were standing, or bending down and peering underneath the carriages, but they could not see anything. As this was the end platform, on the other side of the carriages there was the smoke-grimed wall of the station, with a few gaudy advertisement pictures on it. If Corrissey was under there, he could hide for a long time; but he would have no chance of escaping.

"Sure he's there?" Roger asked Largetson.

"Haven't seen him meself," the other man answered.

"I have, sir." A diminutive porter, with a nose which looked as if it had been pushed to one side, was near them. "A hunchback, he was, came running with a coupla coppers – I—I mean two police officers – running after him. They were too big to get down between the platform and the running-board, but he wasn't."

"Is there any other way out?" Roger asked.

"There are one or two service pits where he could hide, that's all," said the porter, and then he moved aside quickly, for a square-shouldered man in uniform and wearing a peaked cap with some gold braid on it came hurrying. Roger recognised him as the station master; he was affable, although he was burning to get to the fugitive, and shook hands.

"Second time I've had to worry you," he said. "It looks as if the only way we'll flush out the man is to drive the train out. Can you do that without upsetting schedules?"

The station master said dryly: "Lot of difference that will make if you really want it done. But we can move the train twice its own length without interfering with anything. Would you like to be with the driver?"

"No, thanks. I'll watch in case we flush our man."

"A driver's on the way," the station master told him. "Is it this baby-killer case?"

"Yes."

"I hope you don't let the swine escape," the station master said.

Roger made no comment. A brisk-moving man came up, younger than he had expected: the electric train driver. As he made his way towards the front driving cabin, word was passed along to the men on the platform. They stood at intervals of every three or four yards. At the front of the train, more men stood on either side, ready to pounce if Corrissey decided to make a run for it. Roger stood halfway along the platform so that he could see nearly everything, but was blocked by the train itself of the view at the front end on the far side. But once the hunchback was seen, there would be a warning cry, and he would know the truth.

He saw the driver get into his cabin. Almost at once there was a hiss of hydraulic brakes, and then the train began to move, very slowly at first. Every man watched tensely, looking right and left. Roger wished that he were higher up, so that he could get a more comprehensive view, but all he could do was stand there and wait.

The end of the train passed him; in another thirty seconds it would have moved its whole length.

"He's probably clinging to the undercarriage," the station master hazarded. "Or he could be inside one of the carriages, under the seat."

"Every carriage has been entered," Largetson told him. "No, I think—"

Then there came a cry from the far end of the train. *"There he is!"* Roger, already on the move, leapt down on to the track. On the far side, close to the wall, he was able ... to see everything. The hunchback had appeared on the far side, near the front of the train. Four men were closing in on him; it was obvious that he hadn't a chance. Everything was in clear silhouette to Roger; it seemed only a matter of seconds before the wanted man was caught.

Then a man bellowed: "Mind the live rails!"

Everyone who heard that seemed paralysed, even Corrissey; and then everyone began to move with greater care, until Corrissey launched himself at one of the policemen, a hefty man who looked as if he could fell his assailant with a single blow. There was a brief, wild scuffle, and during it an electric train came slowly to a standstill, and instantly Roger realised that the electric current had been switched off. Other men began to move more freely, but before they could reach the two who were struggling, the policeman staggered back, tripped over a rail, and toppled downwards. The hunchback raced through the gap he had made. Men grabbed at him, but missed. Others were shouting. Someone threw a metal object which struck the rails with a crash. The hunchback was now streaking along the track, with men closing in on him from each side.

He dodged to the right, towards the main tracks of the station, and that was the moment when Roger saw the worst danger.

Several trains were coming in, all steam trains, two on the main lines. One was travelling fast, the other crawling. If Corrissey could get between them he would have won a chance for himself. He realised that, and with his head down he ran towards the slow-moving train. Obviously he hoped to get past it, and then to stand between it and the fast-moving train. When that had passed, he could reach the other side of the tracks. There was a wall there, a bridge over the road, and a chance for a man as agile as Corrissey to scramble down. The police were running.

"For God's sake tell them to be careful!" the station master cried. "That train can't stop in time."

"*Stop them!*" Roger shouted. "Largetson! Make sure no one gets hurt."

He was already on the move, towards the slow-moving train and the hunchback. He did not think that he would have a chance to get really near, but had to try. He heard Largetson's voice blaring out over the loudspeaker. "*All police officers stop until the train passes.*" His voice boomed out, but close to the engine of the steam trains the noise was so great that not everyone was likely to be able to distinguish the words. Roger saw most of the men stop, but the two nearest Corrissey went on, and one of them was only three yards behind the man.

Roger was too far away to help.

Corrissey crossed the line in front of the slow-moving train, and then spun round. He hurled something at the two men approaching. Roger saw one of them stop, and fling up his hands, *and trip*. He pitched forward. The other checked his rush, staggered, and then realised how near he was to the train and tried to get back. He succeeded. The first man was lying full length across the rails, and the engine struck him.

He had no chance.

And Corrissey was out of sight, hidden by the carriages of the slow train, while the one which had been moving faster was now slowing down.

The policeman who had been knocked over must have been killed instantaneously. The rage which Roger had felt when he had heard of the finding of Gibson's body was greater now. He was still running, and most of the others had stopped, horrified at their impotence. The man who had just managed to dodge back out of danger was standing motionless, hands raised a little in front of him. Roger saw a foot on the line. A foot. He clenched his teeth and leapt for the running-board of the slowly moving train, reached it, hoisted himself up, and clutched at a door handle. He hauled himself upright. The carriage had four people in it, all of them looking at him, gargoyle-like in their startled stillness. He edged to one side, holding a hand-rail alongside the door and bellowed: "Let me in!"

A man opened the door as the train was jolting to a standstill, and Roger scrambled in and rushed to the corridor. A window was open, and he caught a glimpse of Corrissey crouching between this train and the one alongside it. The one which had been fast moving was now crawling, and Corrissey was close to its last carriage. He did not see Roger and did not look round, but darted behind the train as soon as it passed. He was heading for the signal box, which looked a dazzling white in the sun, and towards the parapet – a kind of bridge over the narrow streets below. Stretched out beyond Roger and the fugitive was the panorama of London, with Big Ben and the Houses of Parliament showing clearly, as if very close to hand.

Corrissey began to clamber over the parapet.

Roger leapt down, and almost fell on to the big flints of the track. He made so much noise that Corrissey glanced over his shoulder and saw him. Until that moment the hunchback had probably believed that he was almost clear.

Roger saw the flint in Corrissey's hand, and as the man flung it Roger ducked, realising what had brought the dead policeman down. He snatched at some of the flints on the track. They were about the size of eggs, and very heavy.

Corrissey was swinging over the parapet, about to climb down. Roger hurled three stones, saw one strike him on the head and bounce off, saw another strike a hand which was clutching the parapet.

The hand was snatched away, and Corrissey fell.

Roger heard nothing, no cry and no thud, until there was a squeal of brakes a long way beneath him. He went to the parapet and looked down. A small private car and a huge lorry were stopping in the road, and the blob that had been Corrissey was between them.

Roger saw the other policeman come up, heard some of them speak to him, and did not speak in return. He felt as if he could fling himself over the parapet, he had made such a hash of this. *Hash.* He kept seeing a mental picture of the policeman being mown down by the train, and seeing Corrissey's face as he had let go of the stonework. He, Roger West, had done everything a man could, had done the only possible thing; yet another policeman had been killed, and he himself had killed a vital witness.

He heard Largetson say roughly: "Shake out of it, Handsome." Largetson's fat fingers were in front of Roger's face, and he snapped forefinger and thumb. Roger moved back from the parapet. Largetson said: "Have a spot of this," and produced a whisky flask. Then he asked, almost savagely: "Is he dead?"

"Yes."

"Damned good riddance."

Roger said: "He was the witness we wanted most."

"All I wanted was to see him dead."

"My God!" Roger exclaimed. "And you're in charge of a Division!"

"And a bloody sight better copper than you are," Largetson retorted.

Roger opened his mouth to snarl back, then realised what he was about to do. No one else was within earshot, but men were looking at them curiously, and if he and Largetson got into a brawl it would be the talk of London's police. He clenched his teeth, and swung away; turning, he saw the little pucker at Largetson's mouth, and swung back.

Largetson was grinning.

"Handsome West back under control," he remarked. "Handsome, don't drive yourself too hard. You always do, you know. Don't carry everybody's blasted burden. It's your one weakness, even if you do want to crown me for telling you about it."

Roger said slowly, gratefully: "Thanks. Let me have a swig of that poison you're carrying." It was whisky. He wiped the back of his hand across his mouth, and said: "Thanks a lot. Mind searching that body for me?"

"I'll fix it," promised Largetson, and then glanced up at someone who was stepping across the rails and frowned. "These baskets seem to have a nose for murder," he went on. "Here's Spendlove of the *Globe*."

Chapter Eighteen

One Step Nearer

Look," Roger said, to Spendlove, "don't push us too far. We'd got all the stations watched and Corrissey, the packing warehouseman at Maddisons, tried to use this one. He tried to escape and jumped to his death. That's it."

"And all about it," Largetson growled.

"Who got nearest to him?" asked Spendlove.

"Wes—"

"A policeman," Roger said. "Policemen do quite a job." He was still edgy, and not quite certain how to deal with this situation; certainly he did not want Largetson to think that he had given the *Globe* man preferential treatment. He found himself thinking that it was odd that Spendlove was so often on the spot; but was it? His job was to follow the case through.

"All right, no more glamour for you," Spendlove responded, good-humouredly. "Any news of that blonde from Maddisons?"

"No. Nor of Cartwright."

"That true that Gibson was rolled up in a carpet?"

"That's guesswork. He might have had a fight in a carpet warehouse, but it doesn't have to be Maddisons. We're checking," Roger said.

"Soft pedal on Maddison, eh?" Spendlove asked, and his eyes seemed to ask the reason for this change of mood on Roger's part.

"They're the right tactics for the moment," Roger said. Then Largetson was called by one of his men, and he was alone with Spendlove. "How did you get to know of this job so soon?"

"We've a chap always on duty at the station," Spendlove answered. "Handsome, I can only go for one thing at a time, and the Great Men said that I must chase that Osborn blonde. I can't find a trace of her. Your chaps have scared the wits out of the girl who shares a flat with her, too. Osborn hasn't turned up at Maddisons, but there's a rumour that she and Edward Maddison were once going together. Did you know that?"

"Rumour is the word," Roger said non-committally. "But there's something you can do. Spread her picture over your newspaper, make a real splash of it. If she's under cover, we want her, and if she's dead—"

"Any reason to suspect that she might be?" Spendlove demanded. He shielded his eyes with one hand against the bright sunlight, and Roger saw how thin and yet tanned it was.

"She took Gibson round. Gibson's dead."

"I see what you mean," conceded Spendlove. "Anything else?"

"I wish you Fleet Street chaps would do your job," Roger said, as if disgruntled. "You ought to have found out that Mrs Shaw, Mrs Kindle and Mrs Graham all worked at Maddisons before they were married."

"God!" exclaimed Spendlove. "And I've been wasting my time on the blonde and Maddison's wife. Want that used?"

"I want anything used that will warn other ex-Maddison employees that there might be a psycho after their children."

"I'll fix it," Spendlove promised. "How about the assistant Corrissey had: Bert May, wasn't it?"

"I'm going to see him and Corrissey's wife now."

He went first to Corrissey's little house. The new widow knew what had happened, and, unless he was badly mistaken, she was stricken with genuine grief. Bert had gone to work, as usual, she said. Roger reached the Mill Street premises nearly two hours after Corrissey's death, was greeted by the white-haired man almost obsequiously, and was taken to the dispatch warehouse at once.

Evans, looking like a ferret, was already there. When Bert May saw Roger, he turned his face away, as if anxious not to be recognised. Roger went to him, made him turn round, and demanded: "Did you help to kill Gibson?"

Bert's face was almost like that of a cretin's. His little eyes were red-rimmed and almost bare of lashes, but their intelligence was clear. His thick lips quivered.

"No, I never," he muttered, and saliva gathered at the corner of his lips. "I told you the truth last night."

"Was he rolled up in a carpet here?"

"I don't know!"

"What about the girl?" Roger flashed.

"Wh—wh—what girl?"

"Miss Osborn. The girl who brought Gibson round here."

"Wh—what do you mean?" demanded Bert, and now there was dismay in the little eyes. "She's all right, isn't she? He told me that she would be all right. *Joe said she would be all right.*"

"Where is she?" Roger demanded.

"I dunno. He told me she was going to hide somewhere for a few days, that was all."

"Tell you what I found," put in Evans, when they were back at the Yard. "A storage bin with some strips of hessian twisted as if they had been knotted. The girl might have been pushed in there, even though May won't admit he knows anything about it."

"What do you make of him?" Roger asked Evans.

"I think he's a lot cleverer and less of a half-wit than he looks," Evans said.

"Better charge him with complicity in Gibson's murder, and bring him here," Rogei said. "We can keep questioning him at intervals. If he really knows anything he will probably break down. Fix it, will you?"

"Yes. Mr West—"

"Yes?"

"I missed that girl at Maddisons."

"I've missed a lot, too."

"What I think ..." Evans said, and then moistened his lips. "What I think is that all this wouldn't have happened at Maddisons unless Edward Maddison knew something about it. He wouldn't let anything go on there that he didn't know about. He was a kind of tyrant there; everybody knows it. If you ask me, he knows where Cartwright is, and knows what's been going on. I think he ought to be pulled in for questioning."

"I had a go at him last night," Roger said. "I want another soon, but I'd like more to go on. That blonde who showed Gibby round once lived with him."

"Well, that's an angle. And he admits that he knew Corrissey hid Cartwright."

"I still want more."

"If you ask me—" Evans began, and stopped as the telephone bell rang. It was just as well; he was irritating Roger, any moment there would have been a sharp order, giving rise to more resentment. Roger picked up the telephone, said curtly: "West speaking," and glanced up at Evans, who was almost sullen. It was a query about a different case, and took only a minute to answer. Roger rang off. "Evans," he said, in a quieter voice, "what's got under your skin?"

Evans answered sourly: "Maddison. He had this *affaire* with the Osborn girl. He's Cartwright's uncle. His own kid's been threatened. Helen Osborn and Cartwright might hate his guts." Evans hesitated, and then threw up his hands. "The truth is I think Maddison's at the bottom of all this, but I can't get a line on him."

"Ledbetter thinks it's Cartwright."

"Why not Cartwright and Maddison working together?" demanded Evans. "Don't ask me what they're working on; I don't know yet. I've got a feeling—"

"Let's have it."

"It's always the same. If I get an idea, I'm slapped down, or else I'm told that someone else has had it. What I really think is that Cartwright's being framed, and Maddison's framing him."

"And I still mustn't ask you why?"

"It's always the same," Evans repeated tautly. "Okay, I'm guessing. But Maddison hid Cartwright and helped to make sure he was hunted, didn't he? Cartwright's cap was found as if it had been planted. Cartwright was just the man to kill the Kindle kid. It's a sight too convenient if you ask me."

So it was, all too obviously, but Roger didn't stop Evans. He had never known the man to talk so freely, never realised that he felt so keenly.

"... what I'm wondering is whether Maddison's still got a love nest somewhere, and Cartwright found it. The old boy's been wenching a lot more than you'd think. If he has a little place tucked away, and the Osborn girl's the bird in the nest – well, it's worth checking, anyway. Might be an angle."

"We'll get on to the love nest angle at once," Roger promised. "I'd been telling myself that framing was out because I couldn't see a motive. You've given me one. Put another two men on to checking Maddison," Roger went on. "Give it priority, concentrate on it yourself, and drop everything else."

When Evans left his cheeks were flushed with mingled excitement and satisfaction.

Almost immediately word came of two mothers with infant children who had worked at Maddisons, one in Fulham, one in Hampstead. Roger arranged for a special watch to be kept on them, sent word to find out if Maddison had ever set his cap at either, and took five minutes off.

It was then half-past three; at least the day hadn't been all bad, for a pattern seemed to be emerging, and leads kept going back to Edward Maddison. Would it still pay to go and see his wife on her own? Would it be a good idea to try to find out if she had any suspicions about a love nest? Roger played with that idea, and rejected it. What he wanted was a fuller history of Hilda Maddison – her own background, friends, habits, enemies, previous boy friends. Supposing Maddison, not Cartwright, was being framed. Maddison could fit the part of victim as easily as that of villain.

Roger put that job in hand with an inspector, and then went to see the girl who shared Helen Osborn's flat.

"Well, yes, she was ever so friendly with Mr Maddison a few years ago, before she shared the flat with me," the girl said. It was a pleasant, three-roomed flat in Kensington. "But when he got married he put all that kind of thing behind him. I'm sure that he never came here to see her. He gave her something, I *think* it was a thousand pounds, for services rendered, you might say, and she was perfectly satisfied. He promised her any easy job for life, too. I don't think there's anything between them now, but I admit that Helen did go off for weekends occasionally without saying where she was going, and it was none of my business, so I didn't inquire. Yes, I suppose she might have seen Maddison; all I can say is that I couldn't be sure …

"Well, yes, she talked about Mr Cartwright sometimes; she thought he was ever so nice. It was a pity that his nose was put out of joint by the baby coming, but Helen wasn't worried about it, I can assure you.

"No, I've no idea at all where she might be. No, she never told me where she was going …"

Roger left the girl at about half-past five, and drove at once to Ledbetter's Divisional office. Ledbetter looked more like a piece of granite than ever, and was scowling, until he saw who it was. Then he sprang up from a swivel chair in a small, scrupulously tidy office, and said: "Trouble?"

"It's all trouble. Have you seen Mrs Kindle today?"

"I've seen our doctor who's seen her, and had one of my chaps talk to her once or twice."

"How is she?"

"Numb."

"Think I can talk to her and get away with it?"

"Shouldn't push her too hard," Ledbetter said, surprisingly. "Otherwise, I don't see why not. What are you after?"

"I'd like to know if she ever had an *affaire* with Edward Madison, and if she did, where," Roger said. "Lend me a guide, will you? I don't want to lose time getting to the house."

Chapter Nineteen

Love Nest?

Roger was surprised to see Anne Kindle looking as if she had rested, and outwardly calm. It was soon obvious that the calm was induced by drugged sleep and shock. Her movements were slow and mechanical. She smiled at him, but it was only a movement of her lips. Her eyes looked as if they had no life. A cousin from the other side of London was with her, a short, dumpy little woman with untidy grey hair and a brisk manner, the kind who would try to make sure that the bereaved mother *did* something. She bustled Roger into the front room, bustled her cousin in after him, and bustled out to say that she was just going to make a cup of tea.

"Mrs Kindle, the last thing I want to do is to worry you," Roger said, "but I'm very anxious to find out who did this dreadful thing."

"I know you are." The voice was as lifeless as the eyes.

"You may be able to help, without knowing it."

"I'll do anything."

"Do you know of anyone who had reason to hate your baby?"

"Not really," she said.

"What exactly do you mean by that?"

"I don't believe that Mr Cartwright would do anything to my baby."

"Did he hate the baby?"

The lack-lustre eyes showed no sign of life.

"He didn't like my baby because I couldn't go out in the evenings, that's all. He always wanted me to go out in the evenings, but how could I? He used to get fed up sometimes, but he wouldn't hurt Nigel. I'm sure he wouldn't."

"Did you ever go out with him?"

"Oh, yes, sometimes."

"Who looked after the baby then?"

"My cousin used to come once a month, and sometimes a lady from next door would sit-in for me."

"I see. And where did you go when you went out with Mr Cartwright?"

"Sometimes to a theatre, and to dinner, sometimes for a drive into the country, and sometimes to the pictures. Somehow I feel that what has happened is a kind of retribution, because a married woman shouldn't go out with a man who isn't her husband, should she?"

"It's very often done, and doesn't always do harm," Roger said, gently.

"A married woman shouldn't," insisted Anne Kindle. "I feel as if it's a kind of vengeance." Still her eyes did not pucker. "I always knew I shouldn't go, and that—that's one of the reasons why I made my baby an excuse. One of the neighbours would always have looked after him for me. I could have gone, but I blamed my baby."

Roger said, softly: "I shouldn't blame yourself at all, Mrs Kindle. And you were alone a great deal, weren't you?"

"Yes."

"When you went into the country for a drive with Mr Cartwright, did you go to any special place?"

"Well, only once," she said, and for the first time feeling crept into her voice. "There wasn't any harm in it."

Roger said: "Are you in love with Roy Cartwright?"

"No!" Again, there was feeling in the voice. "I'm in love with my husband. I always have been; you ought to know that."

"Have you heard from your husband?"

"There hasn't been time," Mrs Kindle protested.

"Did your husband know about your friendship with Roy Cartwright?"

This time Mrs Kindle shouted: "No! And there wasn't any harm in it, not really. I got so lonely here with Jim away for months on end. I couldn't sit in evening after evening. I just couldn't. It was driving me mad. I had to go to the pictures sometimes, I had to talk to someone, I had to dance, and—*now* look what's happened. Now look!"

She began to cry.

Roger heard the sounds of the woman walking about next door, and heard the handle turn. Mrs Kindle was sobbing. The bustler looked up, as if in surprise. A large tea tray was held in front of her, the edge pressing into her bulging bosom.

"Well, you've done more than I could, and I've been trying all day," the bustler declared. "What she wants is a good cry. It's no use bottling everything up inside; you only feel worse. I'll leave the tea, and you can pour out if she quietens down a bit, but don't try to stop her from crying, will you?"

"I won't," Roger promised.

"Come here a minute," said the cousin as she put the tray on a small table. She took Roger's hand and drew him close, and whispered: "Between you and me, she thinks Cartwright did it, but doesn't want to admit it because she thinks it would be partly her fault then. That's her trouble. Conscience. Have you caught the devil yet?"

"No."

"You police take your time, I must say," declared the bustler, and went out.

Mrs Kindle was still sobbing, a heartrending sound. The lid of the metal teapot made a queer little clucking, and kept bobbing and bubbling up. Roger lit a cigarette, smoked it, and poured himself out a cup of tea. He had never needed patience more, yet never been so impatient.

When at last Anne Kindle looked up, her eyes were swimming with tears, all the calmness had gone, her lips were unsteady, her cheeks were wet. She brushed her hands across her eyes, and watched as he poured her a cup of tea, She took it, and began to sip it. All the time she stared at him, and he wondered what was passing through her mind.

Then, abruptly, she said: "I've got to tell someone – if I don't I'll go mad. I didn't do anything wrong with Roy, even when he took me to the bungalow but—but years ago I *did* do wrong with Mr Maddison. I didn't know my husband then, though, and a lot of girls would have done the same. It only happened once. You—you won't tell—"

"Everything you tell me will be in absolute confidence," Roger promised her, and fought to speak gently and convincingly. "Where is this bungalow, Mrs Kindle?"

"I know I shouldn't have, but I was so lonely in those days, and he—he was so good to me," Anne Kindle went on. "We used to go out to a little cottage near Kingston. It was really a little bungalow. I knew I shouldn't, but I didn't seem to be able to help myself. I knew he would marry me if he could, but he was married at the time. Oh, it's awful how things work out. I'd almost forgotten about that when Roy came along. He—he really loves me, I'm sure of that. He *always* wanted to marry me. He said he would do anything in the world if I would get a divorce, but—how *could* I? I was in love with my husband, and—and because of that he's killed my baby."

"Do you really think that Roy Cartwright killed the baby?" Roger asked.

"I don't want to think so, God knows," said Mrs Kindle drearily. "But he hated Nigel, that's a fact. I always told him I couldn't marry him because of Nigel; he was my excuse for not getting a divorce, you see. And – well, Roy got so worked up at times."

"Did he get worked up that night?"

"Yes," she answered, and closed her eyes and turned away, holding her breath. "Yes, that night he said he wished my baby were dead. We had a dreadful quarrel. We had a …"

Roger could not hear the rest of the sentence because she was crying so much. But soon he was asking about the bungalow.

Within twenty minutes, the Surrey police were moving towards the Thames. Roger had been able to give them the address of the riverside bungalow which was nearer Richmond than Kingston, and on a comparatively isolated stretch of the river. Police watched it from the Surrey bank, and approached it from the Middlesex. There were two or three other boathouses and one houseboat within sight, and music was coming from the houseboat when Roger arrived less than an hour after he had left Mrs Kindle. Evans was with him. Evans had discovered nothing new, and had said very little on the way there.

A Surrey superintendent, who looked rather like a retired general, tall, grey-haired, military-looking, greeted Roger briskly.

"Glad to see you again, Superintendent. We haven't met since your promotion. Congratulations."

"Thanks," Roger said. "Any sign of movement at the bungalow?"

"From information received, I understand that a man spends considerable time there on his own, and occasionally a woman goes there with him," said the Surrey superintendent. "I have not been able to ascertain whether he is there tonight or not. At your request, I made sure that no one was given any reason to suspect our interest in the vicinity."

"Thanks," Roger said. "Mind if I go and find out on my own?"

"Glad to co-operate in every way we can," said the Surrey man. "Have you any reason to believe that this man might be armed?"

"I haven't even reason to believe that he'll fight," Roger answered, "but if you and your chaps could get as near as possible without being seen, I'd feel more secure."

"Naturally. And Mr Evans?"

"He'll come with me."

"Very well, Superintendent."

Evans glanced sideways at Roger, looked as if he were going to say 'thanks' and changed his mind. But there was more spring in his step when they got out of the car and walked towards the path which led to the tiny bungalow – little more than an elaborate boathouse. It was badly overgrown with weeds, and there were two patches of bramble where the unsuspecting would tear their clothes, and women would ruin nylons. The only sound came from the houseboat, very distant music, and the soft lapping of water not far away.

They passed a patch of hawthorn, came to the river, broad and slow-moving here, and sparkling. There was a little new-looking bungalow but no sign of movement or of life. By now, the Surrey police were in position, and Roger said: "I'd like you to wait ten feet or so behind me. If he's here, he might be violent."

"More likely he'll cut and run for it," Evans said. There was a narrow door, firmly closed, in the weather-boarding shed of the boathouse section on the river's edge. The path leading to the door was of crazy-paving, and looked as if it had recently been cleared of weeds. Roger's footsteps sounded. He turned the handle of the door and pushed, without expecting it to open. It did not. He put his shoulder to the wood and pressed his weight against it, but would have had to use considerable force to get the door down; and although he had a search warrant in his pocket, he did not want to do any damage if he could avoid it. He saw a small window on one side, went round to it, and peered in. By putting his right hand up against the glass, le could make out the little room inside, the divan bed, a couple of chairs, a small television set and a radio. Beyond his was a doorway, open, and he could see the end of a small boat and thought that there was a small landing stage.

Then, vividly and almost viciously, he was reminded of the running down of the policeman at Waterloo, for he saw man's foot. It was in shadow, and difficult to see, but once he caught sight of it there was no doubt what it was. A man was lying down behind the partition, and the foot lay in a peculiar position, heel against the ground and the toe pointing away from Roger. Only a man dead or unconscious was likely to be so limp as that. Roger swung round.

"Let's get that door down, Evans!" He ran towards the door from one direction and Evans came from the other. Evans reached it first, and charged against it as if his body were a battering ram. He broke the door down first time, and staggered inside. Roger paused to give him time to recover himself, started forward – and then saw Cartwright, who must have been standing behind the door.

Chapter Twenty

Denials

Cartwright gave Evans a push and sent him staggering further into the little room, then sprang out and slammed the door. Roger was only two yards away from him. Cartwright didn't speak. His lips were set tightly and his eyes were glittering. He stood with his back to the doorway which leaned to one side, half-crouching. "Don't play the fool," Roger said. "We want to talk to you."

"Get out of my way."

"You're not helping yourself. Stop behaving like a lunatic."

Cartwright leapt at him from the crouching position. His fists were clenched, he meant to smash Roger down and run for it. Roger swayed to one side, and felt the jolt of a fist against his chin, but it was a glancing blow. He took the next blow on his forearm. There was a moment of furious grappling, and then he got a hold on the other's wrist, twisted, and thrust him backwards. Cartwright gasped in pain. Roger let him go, and he almost fell. Before he could recover, Roger had him in a hammer-lock, facing the doorway as Evans came out. There was a streak of blood on Evans' forehead, and a vicious look in his eyes. He slid his hand into his pocket, and took out handcuffs.

"Let me fix him," he growled, and snapped the handcuffs, fastening Cartwright's right wrist to his own left. Cartwright stood without moving, or attempting to move, staring towards the river. Surrey men came running from the bushes and trees as Roger said:

"Charge him with attempting to inflict grievous bodily harm on a police officer, and attempting to prevent a police officer from carrying out his duty." Evans was just the man for that kind of formality. "Hold him." Roger waved to the Surrey superintendent, who astonished him by whirling along on a bicycle, by far the best and quickest means of transport here.

Then Roger went into the boathouse.

The foot which he had believed to be Cartwright's was still there. If a dead man were behind that door, then Cartwright would really be up against it. He stepped through and looked down at Spendlove of the *Globe*.

The reporter was breathing, and showed no outward signs of injury. Roger moved his right eyelid and saw the pinpoint pupil. He had been drugged with one of the morphia drugs.

There were signs of a struggle inside the little room where Cartwright and Anne Kindle had come from time to time. A chair was on its side, one leg splintered. A bookcase had been knocked to one side, and books had fallen out. Two tumblers were on the floor, one of them broken. Roger saw all this while Spendlove was being carried out of the house into the fresh air. A doctor was already on the way, but Spendlove needed only time to recover from the drug. Cartwright was still handcuffed to Evans, who was standing a few yards from the front door. Two Surrey uniformed men were close by. The 'retired general' was carrying out a more thorough search of the premises; Roger felt sure that he would leave no stone unturned and no avenue unexplored.

"What's Cartwright had to say?" Roger asked Evans.

"Not a word."

Roger studied Cartwright's face for what seemed a long time. Cartwright stared defiantly but without insolence. He was a good-looking man, with lean features and a long jaw. It was easy to believe that he was popular with women, as easy to believe that there was a lot of courage in him. The clear-cut, healthy look was more noticeable out here than 'it had been at Anne Kindle's flat.

"I don't know what this has been about," Roger said, "but if you didn't kill that baby, you'd better talk fast. The quicker we know your side of the story, the better it will be for you."

"I have nothing to say," replied Cartwright.

"Don't be clever," Roger advised. "It never works. You've been charged with two offences which can be proved, and you could go to prison for three years or more for them. That's the least that will happen to you if you don't cooperate."

"I have nothing to say," repeated Cartwright.

"He'll talk when he's cooled his heels a bit," Evans said.

Roger did not feel so sure.

He arranged with the Surrey superintendent to have Evans and Cartwright driven to Scotland Yard, and then went through the boathouse, and checked everything that had been done. Nothing of importance was found. There were only two sets of fingerprints – Spendlove's and Cartwright's. Roger found himself trying to avoid thinking too much about Spendlove, but it would not be long before he began to wonder whether he should take the man on trust. The doctor from Kingston had simply said that he would come round in a few hours. It would not harm him to be driven to London, and he was put into Roger's car, at the back.

"What do you think it amounts to, Superintendent?" inquired the Surrey man. "Do you consider that Cartwright is the baby murderer?"

"It's beginning to look like it," Roger said non-committally.

"Provided there are no other attacks on babies, you should be able to make a fair case," the Surrey man said. "But if there should be another attempt—"

"You couldn't be more right," Roger said.

He knew that it would be in the small hours of the morning before Spendlove came round, and arranged for him to be taken to a small nursing home near the Yard, and for a detective officer to stay at his side. Cartwright was lodged at Cannon Row for the night and would come up on charge in the morning. Bert May would, too. Roger checked that all the precautions of the previous night were being taken again, and Maddison's house was as closely watched as ever. So were the homes of the ex-Maddison staff who had infant children, although neither appeared to have known Maddison, except as the Boss.

Driving away from the Yard, Roger found himself feeling jaded and depressed, in spite of the results. Gibson dead, Corrissey dead, Cartwright caught, only the Osborn girl missing – and they had no real certainty about the killer. He drove out to Esher and saw Maddison alone in the study. Maddison was less intense, and said simply that he had given Roy the keys of the riverside bungalow, which he himself no longer used. He seemed distressed about Corrissey, and seemed to assume that the hunchback had panicked when he had realised that Gibson was dead.

"Have you any reason to believe that Corrissey had any motive for killing these babies?" Roger demanded.

"I simply cannot imagine anyone with a motive for such hideous crimes," Maddison said.

When Roger reached home, the boys were squatting in front of a family programme on the television, and although they jumped up the moment he came in, obviously they were interested mostly in the screen. Janet was sitting beneath a wall lamp, reading a newspaper, and she looked up brightly when he entered, scanning his face for an indication of how things had gone.

She would know about Gibson, of course.

"Come into the kitchen while I get supper," she said, "I can't get the boys away from the television tonight. Sometimes I could throw the thing out of the window."

Scoop heard that, and looked round.

"Is there anything I can do, Mum?"

"Just say if there is," urged Richard, without looking round.

"I'll call you in a minute," Janet said.

The kitchen was bright, and spick and span. Roger sat in an old Windsor armchair, took out cigarettes, and watched Janet as she busied herself with steak and chips. The potatoes hissed and spat as they fell into the boiling fat, the steak sizzled and hissed under the grill, Janet laid a place at the corner of the small kitchen table, and waited for Roger to speak.

"If we get through the night without an alarm, I'll begin to believe that Cartwright's really our man," he said. "At least we've got him. If we do have another alarm—"

"Think we shall?"

"I haven't made up my mind what to think," Roger admitted. "I'm just not satisfied that we've got all the answers yet."

There was no alarm during the night.

There was a message, at eight o'clock next morning, saying that Spendlove had recovered at about five o'clock, but insisted on making a statement to Roger only.

Spendlove looked a little pale and his eyes were dull, as if he had a headache; but there was nothing the matter with his mood. He was fully dressed and sitting in an armchair. The detective who had been with him all night was now on his way back to the Yard with a report; and would then go home. Spendlove was smoking a cigarette, and smiling one-sidedly as Roger stood and studied him.

"Not guilty," he said.

"I'd like to make sure," retorted Roger. "How did you get into that bungalow?"

"I'd done work on Maddison before, and had discovered that at one time he'd owned a little riverside love nest. It didn't take too long to find where, and I went to see if Cartwright was there, by any chance, and whether Helen Osborn had an *affaire* with him, too."

"Any reason to think that she had?"

"I've no reason to think anything, except that Cartwright, isn't a man I'd like to meet on a dark night. He found me snooping round, and before I knew where I was he'd hauled me inside, and laid about me. I don't know whether you're disappointed, but I was never a physically courageous man," Spendlove went on. "That's another reason why I didn't join the police force."

"What did Cartwright do?"

"Floored me, and said that he would beat me to pulp if I didn't tell him why I was there. So I told him everything – or nearly everything – that I've told you. I did it in such a way that I got him to tell me some of the answers I wanted. When the session was over and he thought he had everything he wanted, he gave me a glass of beer with a couple of morphine tablets in it. He actually told me what they were and said that if I didn't take them he would ram them down my throat. I was sure he meant it."

"Did you try to stop him?"

"Handsome, I made two attempts to get out, one by the front door and one by the river, and he stopped me each time." Spendlove rubbed his chin gingerly. "I don't mind admitting that I wasn't sure whether I was with a killer or not, and I didn't like to take a chance. I've never been so terrified as when I took those tablets, either; for all I knew, he was giving me a lethal dose. He said that he wanted to make sure that I couldn't put you on to him until the morning, when he'd had a chance to finish what he was trying to do."

"Did he tell you what he was trying to do?"

"Yes," answered Spendlove. "It's so corny that even you will find it hard to believe."

Roger said easily: "I can tell you, I think. He says he has been and is being framed for the murder of Anne Kindle's baby. He believes this is all part of a plot to get him out of the family firm. His uncle and, possibly, his aunt by marriage, are setting out to ruin him. How am I doing?"

Spendlove took out cigarettes, proffered them, flicked his lighter and, when they were both smoking, answered wryly: "You forget one thing."

"Wait a minute, and I'll try to remember it," Roger said. "I imagine that it has something to do with his uncle employing a scoundrel like Corrissey, who actually murdered the baby, timing it so that he, Cartwright, would look as guilty as hell."

"Right on the nose," Spendlove agreed, admiringly. "All right, Handsome. That's the explanation that I had to listen to. It's a peculiar thing," went on the newspaperman, after a pause, "but as you told it to me and as I would tell it to you, it sounds phoney. In fact it sounds quite unbelievable. It's a pity you didn't hear Cartwright telling the tale. I don't know whether he would have convinced you, but he came very close to convincing me."

"What made him so persuasive?"

"It's hard to say," Spendlove answered. "It was partly the way he told the story, I suppose. He knew that, if he were arrested, charges would be made; and he didn't think he had a chance. He was sure that his uncle was behind the framing and he wanted to find the proof. The only way was to find Corrissey and force him to talk. As a matter of fact," went on Spendlove, "I think that's the real explanation of my being fooled into believing him. He didn't know that Corrissey died yesterday."

"Did you tell him?"

"Yes. It knocked him badly, too. He was going after Corrissey because he believed he could make him talk. Now he doesn't think anyone can help him."

"Did he say anything about the Osborn girl?"

"She was there when he ran from the dispatch room."

"Did you ask if he knows where she went?"

"Believe me, I did. He said he ran for the vans and hid in one which soon moved off, and didn't see the blonde again." Spendlove finished his cigarette and stubbed it out in a porcelain ash tray. "I don't think you'll get him to talk, now. I think he'll believe that the dice are loaded against him, and he would only be wasting his time."

"We'll see about that," Roger said. "Is that the lot?"

"Everything."

"You may have to say so in court."

"And it won't be perjury."

"Right!" said Roger briskly. "Now I'll be going. I'll tell the chap outside that you can go when you want to. Only next time there's trouble, don't be in the middle of it, will you? First at Anne Kindle's place. Then at the warehouse. Then at the river. Next at the station. And yesterday at the river bungalow. Once more would be just too much for coincidence."

"You were there, too," Spendlove retorted, "and we've the same kind of job even if we do it in different ways."

"As you pointed out once before," Roger said.

"Handsome, if you think that I'm involved—" Spendlove began, but before he could finish, the door opened and Evans appeared.

Roger had not seen him this morning, and had only once seen him with the flushed cheeks and the bright eyes that he had now.

Spendlove shut his mouth like a trap.

Evans said: "Hilda Maddison's just had another threat against her baby's life. *That* wasn't made by Cartwright, Corrissey or Bert May, was it?"

At the Esher house, Hilda was beside herself, and no one could pacify her. She would not let the child out of her sight.

Chapter Twenty-One

Defence in Depth

"Well, anyway, there can't be any danger to the kid," Evans declared to Roger.

At the end of The Close there had been two police cars and two men in plain-clothes, as well as the drivers. Halfway along, two men had been working on an electric cable in the road, and a uniformed policeman was with them. By the front gate were two more Divisional officers, and yet another was in the porch of the lovely house, which Roger saw for the first time in daylight. The fact that there were so many policemen about distracted his attention from the long, low building, with a Norfolk thatch roof, the beautifully-leaded windows, the oak beams and the ornamental garden. A small fountain was playing in the middle of a lawn which looked as if it had been brought from the quadrangles of Oxford. Apart from the waiting, watching men, there was quiet everywhere, except that a long way off a lawnmower clattered.

Roger and Evans walked up to the front of the house, and a local C.I.D. man came from the hall.

"Is Maddison here?" asked Roger.

"There was a telephone message ten minutes ago, to say that he's on his way."

"How's his wife?"

"Absolutely distraught," the other man answered. "She won't let the baby go out of her sight for a moment. Her doctor's with her. The housekeeper sent for him."

"Sounds the sensible thing to do," Roger said, and then the door opened and a brisk, elderly man came hurrying down the drive, peering shortsightedly at Roger. Roger, unexpectedly, grinned at him, and the doctor said: "Well, well! It's Mr West. How are you?" They shook hands. "I hope you don't allow this case to drag on much longer; that young woman will collapse. I can't even persuade her to take aspirins. She's afraid that if she sleeps for five minutes the child might be hurt."

"We won't be a minute longer than we have to," Roger said. ,

"Sure you won't. How's your wife?"

"Fine, thanks."

The doctor went off, nodding, and Roger looked up at the policeman by his side.

"The first time we met he hated my guts," he explained. "I was on a job in which some patients of his were suspects. They weren't guilty, so ... that's beside the point. Are you making sure that no one goes near the house?"

"You bet I am. All the tradespeople leave the goods at the back gate, with our chaps."

"Checking baby foods for poison?"

The local man said: "God!"

"Better get everything checked in a hurry, and get hold of some sealed and tinned foods for present use," Roger said briskly. "We ought to have sugar, packets of baby foods, dill-water, Milk of Magnesia, all unsealed goods that might be given to the baby."

"She'll never let you go near the stuff!"

"We'll see," said Roger.

The front door was closed. As he approached, the policeman rang the bell, but there was no answer. He rang again when Roger drew up, and said under his breath: "She won't even let the servants answer."

"Has anyone been in since the threat was received?"

"Yes, sir, she allowed the first detectives who called to come in, and then locked the door. I don't know how—"

There was the sound of a car turning the corner. Roger looked round, not surprised to see a Rolls-Royce. It came smoothly along the road, with a chauffeur at the wheel, and Maddison sitting in the back and leaning close to the window, as if he could not get the door open fast enough. The moment the car stopped, the door was thrust open, and Maddison leapt down and began to run towards the gate. Roger stood on the porch, surprised by the older man's agility, if not by the expression of alarm on his face. A policeman opened the gate, and Maddison came through as if he had not realised that it had been there. He had a hand at his hip pocket, and by the time he reached the porch, had his keys in his hand. Roger stood to one side, and Maddison thrust a key towards the door, saying: "Is my wife all right?"

"As far as I know."

"What the devil do you mean, as far as you know?" growled Maddison. "Isn't that what you're supposed to do? Protect citizens?" The key caught, he thrust at it, and muttered under his breath; the door opened and he hurried inside. Roger went after him, caught his shoulder, pulled him back and stood in front of him.

"If you don't let me pass—" Maddison began.

"Quiet!" Roger ordered. And then he called: "Are you there, Mrs Maddison?"

There was a pause; and silence.

"Hilda!" cried Maddison.

For a dreadful moment Roger thought that, in spite of the precautions, someone had got in, had reached the mother and her child, and had struck them down. It was by far the worst moment he had known. Then, a door at the end of the hall opened, and a heavily-built man appeared.

"Where is your mistress?" demanded Maddison tautly.

"She—she's locked herself in her bedroom with the baby, and won't come out, sir. She ordered us not to let anyone in, and not to answer any telephone calls."

Roger was already halfway up the stairs, heart pounding, fears increasing. He tried the handle of the main bedroom door but the door would not budge. Maddison came just behind him, calling out: "Hilda! Hilda, open the door!" There was a moment of silence before Maddison rattled the handle and shook the door wildly.

It opened.

Hilda Maddison stood holding the side of the door. Beyond her was a lovely room, with the curtains drawn and the blinds down. Behind her was the cot, and she sheltered it with her body, as if determined to make sure that no one could get near it without passing her. She had no vestige of colour, except at her lips and eyes; and her eyes looked startlingly blue.

"Are you all right? Is Charles—"

"Don't let that man come near me," Hilda said shrilly. "Don't let anyone come near baby. Someone is going to kill him – they said so on the telephone again. Someone is going to kill him!"

Maddison stepped past her towards the cot, and stood gripping it and staring down; his lips were working, and he seemed to be gasping for breath. His wife, still defensively, was watching Roger and there was no doubt that if he made a move to pass her she would fly at him. The strange brightness of her eyes and the tension of her lips gave her a ferocious expression; a maddened beauty.

Roger said sharply: "Mr Maddison, I don't want the child to have any food that is now in the house. Everything – milk, powders, and medicines – must be brought in sealed. I will arrange for a policewoman to come here to prepare the food and act as nurse until the emergency is over."

Maddison swung round. "Do you seriously think—"

"It's a possibility and must be checked. All the foods now in the house are to be sent to an analyst at once. Have you any idea who threatened the child?"

"No. I had a message from my wife – that is all."

"Was it from a man or a woman, Mrs Maddison?"

The woman did not seem to hear him.

"Hilda! You must tell us who telephoned."

"Was it a man or was it a woman?" Roger demanded.

"Woman?" Maddison echoed.

"Answer me, please," Roger said roughly. "If we're to find out who it was, we've got to be quick." "Hilda—"

"It was a woman," Hilda Maddison answered. "It was a woman, and she said—"

"Step up the search for Helen Osborn," Roger ordered Evans. "Call the Yard, and ask them to call all London and Home Counties police stations, give a new description of her, alert all stations, ports and airfields. Then try to find out if she was associated with Cartwright as well as with Maddison."

"Right," Evans said, and hurried down the path towards the police cars.

Roger turned back to the house, where the Maddisons were still upstairs. The elderly servants came from the kitchen together, a little alarmed and put out because food was being taken away by the police.

"If we're not trusted—" the woman began. She was bigger even than her husband, and had a remarkably lined face.

"It's not a question of not trusting you," Roger said. "Anyone could have come to the house and poisoned some food without you or anyone else knowing it. If I were you I would carry on as normally. After it's all over, you'll be all right."

"That's all very well, but—"

"When did Mrs Maddison first begin to show fear about the baby?" Roger asked.

"Oh, it was only a few days ago," the ex-policeman answered eagerly.

"Was there any special reason? Had anyone been to see her, or had she had a telephone call or a letter?"

"I *think* it was something she read in a newspaper," the woman answered.

"When did you first find that she was afraid of Mr Cartwright?"

"Oh, that wasn't until yesterday, when his name was in the newspapers."

"Thanks," said Roger, and went upstairs to meet Maddison coming out of the bedroom. Through the open door, Hilda Maddison was visible, sitting by the cot. Maddison looked pale and shaken and old; much of the alertness seemed to have gone from his face.

Roger said: "Can you spare me a few minutes alone, sir?"

"Yes," agreed Maddison, in a low-pitched voice. "Yes, of course. Come into my study." It was a small, beautifully furnished room, overlooking the back garden, with the fine lawns, a magnificent herbaceous border, and a fountain on one side. "Sit down, Mr West."

Roger didn't move, but asked roughly: "Have you heard from Helen Osborn today?"

"No."

"Do you know if your nephew and Helen Osborn were associated in any way?"

"What?"

Roger didn't repeat the question.

"Good God, no!" Maddison exclaimed. "In fact Roy resented her very much indeed, just as much as he resented my marriage. I believe that he always suspected that I might marry Helen, and he was always aware of the fact that my marriage to anyone could affect his own future, although of course that would be affected only by issue of the marriage." He was sitting back in an easy chair, still very pale, and his eyes narrowed, as if he had an almost unbearable headache. "Roy disliked Helen intensely. I suppose—" He pressed his hands against his forehead, paused, then went on as if with great effort: "I suppose it would be better if—if it turned out to be Helen rather than Roy. But I don't know what my wife will do if she should ever find out that this happened because of that old *affaire*."

There was no useful comment to make.

"Have you seen Helen Osborn recently outside the office?"

"No," said Maddison. "I haven't been back on the old footing with her there, either. As my secretary, she had a sinecure – and often the very pleasant job of showing customers round, taking them out to a meal occasionally; she couldn't have had a better job. I can hardly believe—" He broke off, squared his shoulders again, and went on: "It won't help if I talk like that. Mr West, how can we take this awful threat away? What can we do? What chance is there of your finding Helen? Haven't you *any* idea where she is?"

"No," Roger answered, "but I think there's a way that we can find out – if she did make the threat and is determined to try to harm the baby."

"How?" Maddison demanded, and gripped his shoulder tightly. "Tell me how."

Chapter Twenty-Two

Ruse

"We can only do it with your co-operation and with your wife's," Roger said, "and I don't think that Mrs Maddison will want to work with us."

"I'll make sure that she does," Maddison assured him. "Are you sure it will succeed?"

"As soon as your nephew was under arrest, this new threat was made," Roger reminded him. "That showed a defiance and a kind of bravado more likely in a psychopath than from a person who is normal, and doing this for a coldblooded motive. We can't take that or anything else for granted yet – the man might be trying to persuade us that he's not sane. But either way, if he believes that the child is unprotected, he's likely to try again."

"Have you taken leave of your senses?" demanded Maddison harshly.

Roger said: "I should keep your voice down, sir. It isn't uncommon after an arrest has been made to have someone quite unconnected with the crime telephone and say that lie knows all about it. If in this case we let it be generally believed that we're sure we have the right man in your nephew, and that we're taking off the guard—"

"But you can't be sure!"

"No, but we can pretend that we are," Roger said patiently. "The Press will co-operate in every way. We have reasonable grounds for charging Mr Cartwright with the murder of the Kindle baby. If we do that, then the newspapers will report it in such a way that the general public will believe that no one else is involved. We can make sure that the newspapers say that the house is no longer being especially guarded. That is where we shall need your wife's co-operation, although there's a risk that we won't get it."

"Do you mean you want to provoke an attempt on my child?" Maddison demanded, incredulously.

Roger thought: He must have a mind or else he's just playing dumb. He said aloud: "I want to provoke an attack on this house, sir. Your child would be removed to a place of safety, of course."

Maddison frowned. Roger didn't go on, and suddenly the other man's expression cleared, and he said: "Of course! I quite see the point. I'm afraid that I'm not myself, Mr West. The child will be taken away but the attacker will believe that he is still in the house. Yes, of course, but – can you be sure that everyone will believe that?"

"We can try," Roger said.

"I can see the possibilities," Maddison conceded slowly. "If your men are withdrawn, if the newspapers imply that you believe there is no further danger, then the killer is likely to think it safe to come. Yes." He began to smile a little tensely. "I understand why you have a reputation for unorthodoxy, Mr West. As you rightly say, the great stumbling block will be my wife, and I think that the best thing will be to make sure that she has a sedative at the crucial time. I can arrange that – Dr Fisher left tablets for her. I shall stay home for a day or two, or would it be better if we were to go away with the baby?"

"You've got to live here, and you've got to behave normally," Roger said.

"Ah, yes. Of course. Shall we dismiss the nurse and the staff?"

"If you do, it will look as if you think there's still danger," Roger argued. "They must believe that the baby is still here, so we've got to smuggle him out. If the newspapers come out with the story tomorrow morning, the best time to deal with your wife and to bring the baby away will be about ten o'clock. Is that all right with you?"

"Perfectly all right," Maddison said, now almost eager. "Do you expect an attack immediately?"

"If it isn't made before your wife comes round we'll have to think up another one," Roger said dryly.

"At least you've given me some cause for hope," declared Maddison.

Roger made no comment, but went out of the house soon afterwards. A police car with a tray containing baby foods was being driven away. A crowd of a hundred people or more was watching, and the end of the street was almost blocked with cars, with the police trying to make sure that the traffic was kept on the move. A path was made for Roger's car. He drove straight to the High Street, and stopped outside a small Georgian house, with brass plates on the gate; one announced Dr C. Fisher. He saw Fisher's Rover by the garage and within two minutes was standing with a whisky in his hand, while the doctor said: "Here's to your success, West."

"Cheers," Roger said, and drank. "Ah, I needed that! I've really come to ask if you think it will be safe to—"

He told Fisher what he proposed, and how Hilda Maddison would be treated. Fisher nodded both comprehension and approval.

"That's all right. Good idea, I should think."

"Thanks. Have you known Maddison long?"

"Most of my life."

"Is he quite normal?" Roger asked bluntly.

Fisher hesitated, and then asked: "In what way might he be abnormal?"

Roger said bluntly: "I could understand a lot more than I do if Maddison was sterile in the sense that he couldn't become a father. Is he?"

Fisher said quietly: "You can't expect me to break a patient's confidence, West."

"Keeping it might condemn another patient to death." When Fisher didn't answer, Roger grinned unexpectedly. "A nod being as good as a wink, I'll call that a day. Is the child Maddison's?"

Fisher answered gruffly: "No. The mother's terrified of the truth coming out. I'm one of the few men alive who know that her baby can't be his. I knew his first wife, you know, before she died in a car accident; she always longed for a child. West, don't let harm come to the baby."

Roger said, tensely: "Not if I can help it." He felt a kind of exhilaration which often came when he believed that he was near the end of a case, sat back at his desk, alone, with all the notes in front of him, and made fresh ones about Cartwright, Helen Osborn, Spendlove and the Maddisons, especially this latest piece of information. He was glancing through reports which had come in while he had been out, and was brought up sharply when he read:

Telephone message from AS Division: Mrs Graham recalls that the Maddison warehouse labourer, May, was devoted to her, also to Mrs Shaw (nee Barber) and Mrs Kindle (nee Blythe). He was also devoted to Helen Osborn.

Bert May looked vacant when Roger went across to him at the cells at Cannon Row police station, and puzzled when Roger said: "Do you want to spend the rest of your life in prison, May?"

"No, sir, I certainly don't."

"Then tell me the truth, without wasting any more time."

"But I have, sir," May insisted. "I don't know nothing about them babies, I swear I don't."

"You knew their mothers," Roger said. "Do you remember Joyce Barber?"

The man's eyes lit up momentarily, but the light quickly faded.

"And Anne Blythe?" went on Roger.

"I—I don't know what you mean!" Bert muttered. "Why do you ask me all these questions?"

"Why did you want to hurt these women?"

"I never hurt them!"

"Killing their babies hurt them, didn't it? And killing Helen Osborn hurt her, didn't it?" Roger demanded in a stony voice.

"I didn't, I saved her!" cried the labourer. "Corrissey would have killed her, and I saved her. Why, I let her go. She promised faithfully not to talk and make trouble."

This was much better.

"Where is she now?" Roger demanded.

"I don't know, I tell you. If I don't know, I can't tell you, can I?" May's voice was strident in his vehemence. "Corrissey was going to kill her because she had seen him attack that policeman who came for Mr Cartwright, but I saved her!"

Once he had started to talk, the rest was easy. He confessed to everything he had done, but insisted that he had no idea where Helen had gone, and no idea why Corrissey had helped Cartwright to escape. Whether he was lying or not, he no longer pretended to be half-witted. He admitted under very little pressure, that he had idolised all the attractive girls at Maddisons. A few had known of that, and apparently all had been compassionate because he had seemed pathetic in his devotion. He swore that that was all.

He might still be protecting Helen Osborn, Roger knew; there was no way of being sure.

Roger returned to his office, and first checked the charges which could be brought against Roy Cartwright. There was sufficient in what had happened on the night of the Kindle baby's murder to charge him with that on circumstantial evidence. Hardy would prefer something stronger, but would almost certainly give Roger his support. The Assistant Commissioner was away, so Hardy would be the man to decide. Roger telephoned him, and Hardy said: "I've got to go along to the Commissioner's office, Handsome. Can't we fix this by telephone?"

"I want to charge Cartwright with the Kindle baby's murder."

"Got new evidence?"

"No, but—"

"You'd better handle it the way you think best," said Hardy, "but don't lay yourself open to too strong an attack from Maddison. He's been trying to pull strings at the Home Office today."

"He won't try to pull any more," Roger said grimly. "Thanks. I'll keep you posted."

He went downstairs to the waiting-room where Cartwright was being held. There was a uniformed policeman outside the door and another just inside. Cartwright was sitting by the barred window, looking out into the courtyard, where Flying Squad cars and private cars were parked, and where Yard men were continually on the move. It was just possible to see the traffic in Parliament Street, beyond Cannon Row. Cartwright stood up when Roger entered, and declared: "I've already made it clear that I have nothing more to say."

"Please yourself," Roger said. Evans came in at that moment, with the look of excitement about him which had been evident since the affair at the riverside. "Is your name Roy Montgomery Cartwright?" went on Roger.

"Don't be a fool. You know it is!"

"Roy Montgomery Cartwright, it is my duty to charge you with wilfully causing the death of an infant, to wit Nigel Arthur Kindle, on the night of May the third, and to inform you that anything you say may be taken down in writing and used in evidence," Roger said formally.

Cartwright seemed to wilt.

Evans' eyes glowed.

"Have you anything to say?" Roger asked.

Cartwright said: "You're a bigger fool than I thought you were. My uncle killed them. He's as mad as a coot in some ways. If Corrissey were alive I'd make him talk; that's what I knew I'd have to do. My uncle and he fixed this devilry between them."

"Are you guessing, or have you any proof?" demanded Roger.

"If I had proof I wouldn't be here," Cartwright said bitterly.

Roger left him, and went to the Back Room, the small office near the Embankment where a chief inspector dealt with releases for the Press. Sitting in the small waiting-room were half a dozen men in addition to Aunt Martha, who had a benign matronly look, and smiled brightly at him. As if knowing that he had arrived, as many reporters then outside on the Embankment thronged in.

"I'm sure you're going to tell us that it's all settled and done with," Aunt Martha cooed. "It would be very nice if we could have a statement like that without Spendy knowing in advance, wouldn't it?"

"Now don't rub Handsome up the wrong way," someone called out.

"Impossible today," Roger rejoined. "If Spendlove gets on the spot before you do, whose fault is it? I didn't come to see you people, anyhow, I came to see Nebby."

The Chief Inspector in charge said: "It's all yours, Super."

"Can we quote you, Superintendent?" inquired Aunt Martha.

"Yes," said Roger briskly. "We have just charged Roy Montgomery Cartwright with the wilful murder of the Kindle baby. He will be in court in the morning. We shall offer only formal evidence of arrest and ask for a remand in custody. That much is official. If you'd like one or two oddments off the record—"

"What do *you* want, that's more to the point," said Aunt Martha.

"I want a piece on every front page on the lunatics who utter threats after an arrest has been made," Roger said. 'Cartwright's arrest this afternoon was in the early evening papers, and within an hour the Maddison's baby had been threatened. We found who did it – someone who is half mad all the time. But you can take it from me that we're not worried about the Maddison child, and we're not keeping any special watch after tonight." Eyes were glistening.

"Why tonight?" demanded Aunt Martha. "If the danger's over, why not withdraw your men right away?"

"Because Mrs Maddison has been almost frantic with anxiety," Roger answered. "We don't want to be too abrupt."

"Kind-hearted Scotland Yard," scoffed Aunt Martha. She did not join the scramble to get to the telephones, but waited until Roger and the Back Room inspector were alone, and then asked in her familiar, cooing voice: "Sure it was Cartwright, Handsome?"

"How often have you known me make an arrest before I've got a case?"

"I don't really know," said Aunt Martha thoughtfully. "I wouldn't put anything past you. You didn't tip Spendy off about this first, did you?"

"I did not."

"Have you found Helen Osborn yet?"

"No."

"Expecting to find her alive?"

"Let's say I'm hoping to," Roger said, and then glanced up and saw Spendlove come in. He looked more pale than usual and his eyes were lack-lustre, but he found a grin for Roger and Aunt Martha.

"There seems to be some excitement," he observed. "What's it all about?"

"Handsome has decided not to have favourites anymore," said Aunt Martha. "Handsome, if there's a word more in the *Globe* than you've told us, we shall start a campaign against you, and say that it's time the Yard's glamour boy stopped talking out of turn." Her smile was hardly benevolent as she went out.

"She always was the smartest of the lot," said Spendlove. "I had a word with one of our chaps outside – they'd sent a message that you were in the Back Room. Hi, Nebby – is West pinching all the limelight again?"

"As usual," said the Back Room inspector.

"That right it was Cartwright?" Spendlove asked.

"It looks as if he was fooling you," said Roger. "He's been charged, and I don't think we'll have any more trouble."

"I hope you're right," Spendlove said. He spoke almost as if he knew that this move was a ruse, and that Roger was a long way from being sure of himself.

"You got him, then," Scoopy said eagerly at breakfast next morning. "I always thought it was Cartwright, but you weren't so sure, were you?"

"Of course he was, only he didn't let you see it. *I* could tell," Richard declared.

"What a relief that poor mother must be feeling," Janet said, as she came in with the frying pan in one hand, and a sausage at the end of a fork in the other. "Hurry up, Richard, you're always last. Like a piece more fried bread, Scoop?"

"Ooh, yes, please!"

Roger said: "You spoil him, that's the trouble."

He rang the Yard, puzzling the boys by asking for two identical suitcases, very light in weight and with ventilation holes in them, to be available for him round the corner from Maddison's house; then, leaving the boys mystified, he drove to Esher. Only one or two policemen were in sight, and these seemed bored; there was none of the excitement that there had been the previous evening. After putting the cases in his car, Roger went straight to the front door carrying one of them, and the middle-aged ex-policeman opened it immediately.

"Mr Maddison is expecting you, sir," he greeted, and led the way upstairs.

Maddison came hurrying out of his study. Obviously he had slept quite well, and he looked more youthful; the age gap between him and his wife no longer seemed almost absurd.

"I gave my wife a special sleeping draught, which Dr Fisher sent round, with her morning tea, Mr West, and she is asleep now. I know from experience that she will sleep for at least six hours. And I have arranged for my car to be here in half an hour. For safety's sake I will take the baby – who has also had a mild sedative – and you will be here to make sure that you catch anyone who comes. There can't be any slip now, can there?"

"None at all," Roger said. "Except—"

"If there can be, tell me what it is," Maddison demanded. He was impatient and arrogant as well as eager. "I've gone to great trouble, even to the extent of drugging my wife, in order to make sure that there is no more danger. Don't tell me that you aren't sure now!"

Roger said: "I'm quite sure, Mr Maddison, but I don't want you to take the child."

"What on earth do you mean?"

"I want one of my men—"

"Don't be absurd!" barked Maddison. "No one will know that I have the baby with me. I shall take a small case – this one here," he added, and pointed to an overnight valise. "That is what I carry my papers and books in to and from the office. No one will suspect that my child is in it, and there is ample room – I have laid the baby inside the case once already, to make sure. If you think that I am going to allow anyone else to have the custody of the child, you are quite wrong."

Roger said: "Very well, Mr Maddison, on one condition."

"You are in no position to impose conditions."

"I shouldn't force that issue," Roger said dryly. "It's very simple – the child must go in this case." He held up the one he had brought. "All my men have a description of it, in case anything goes wrong."

"Oh, very well," said Maddison. "I am glad that you agree that only a father has the right to take care of his own child. I shall go straight to the City. Armchairs in my office will be used as a cot. It is not uncommon for me to instruct everyone to stay outside while I concentrate and that is what I shall do today. No one but I will know that the child is with me, Mr West. From that point of view, nothing at all can go wrong. From yours – have you any idea where the young woman is?"

"I think you can be sure that an attempt will be made on the child at the house," Roger said, "and that we shall make an arrest this morning."

"Do you think my nephew was involved in it?"

"I think I would rather await events, sir."

"Very well," said Maddison again. "Now I'll go in and see my wife. Will you be present when I take the child?"

"Yes," Roger answered.

"I can't see why you're so certain," Evans said, almost sharply. "I agree it might work, but you've stuck your neck right out, Handsome. Supposing no one does come here today?"

Roger grinned.

"No one will," he said. "You switch those cases, so that we have the baby safe, and Maddison has one with a bundle in it. Even if I'm wrong, no harm will be done then. We'll follow the Rolls-Royce in a van. The attack, if that's the word, will be on the Rolls, not on the house. Come on."

"But—"

"I'm making sure that the Rolls is delayed round the corner to give us time to get on its tail," Roger said. "Let's hurry."

Chapter Twenty-Three

Last Attempt

"If you expect the Rolls to be attacked, why the hell did you lay all this on?" Evans demanded, as they got into the plain blue van which had radio and a super-charged engine.

"Because I had to fool the killer," Roger answered. "And if I'd fixed everything I'm fixing now any earlier there might have been a leak of information. Spendlove has been learning too much, and I suspect there's a leak at the Yard – nothing serious, but enough to risk our man getting a warning."

"Do you think Spendlove—" Evans began, but Roger had flicked a switch, and began to talk to Information, at the Yard.

"In about ten minutes Edward Maddison will be leaving his home in his Rolls-Royce car, a black 1959 Silver Wraith. He will be driving himself, and his child will be in a brown fibre-board case beside him. I want him followed by at least two of our cars. Its route is likely to be straight to the Kingston by-pass and, if it gets that far, to Roehampton, Putney, Fulham, then along the Embankment. I expect some kind of attack on the Rolls-Royce, probably in the form of an accident. I've asked for the co-operation of all Divisional and Surrey police, to have radio-equipped police cars at all likely spots for an accident. I shall be following in a garage service van, a Commer, registration number 8JE 12. Let me have freedom of movement everywhere. Is that all clear?"

Evans was staring at him as if he had gone mad. "All clear, sir," Information said.

"Thanks." Roger rang off, and grinned at Evans. "I know," he said. "And don't take the huff because I didn't tell you about this beforehand. I didn't tell a soul." He drove his own car towards the centre of Esher, parked it in a side street behind the repair van he had told Information about, and took the wheel of the van. He sat watching the driving mirror, with Evans saying nothing, but looking out of the window from time to time. He exclaimed: "Here it comes!"

Roger let in the clutch. The repair van with a specially tuned engine slid into the road fifty yards ahead of the Rolls-Royce. Traffic lights were green for it, but held up the other car. Roger turned towards the Kingston by-pass and reached the roundabout beyond Haydock Park at least a hundred yards ahead of the Rolls-Royce.

Evans said: "What are we looking for?"

"A car to bump into the Rolls-Royce almost certainly on the passenger's side, or in the rear," Roger said. "It won't be a big smash. The baby will be snatched from Maddison's side, and Maddison will probably appear to be knocked out."

"How the hell do you know?"

Roger said: "It's inevitable, if I'm right about the people and the motives." He did not slow down, but the Rolls-Royce came sweeping behind him. It would pass before they reached the next roundabout. Roger saw a police car pulled up at one side, and knew that a radio report would be made as soon as the Rolls-Royce passed. He watched all the side turnings intently and, as he approached roundabout after roundabout, watched the right-hand side for any car which might swing into the Rolls-Royce.

Nothing did.

Evans asked out of the blue: "Do you think it *is* Mad—" A sports car swung round a corner towards the Rolls, and for a moment it looked as if it would crash into the rear. Maddison appeared to be oblivious. The driver of the car, young and fair-haired, jammed on his brakes in time to miss the other car by a hair's-breadth, grinned, and drove on.

"Gawd!" groaned Evans.

"You'll get used to it," Roger said.

A Jaguar swept up from behind the van, and passed. The driver was a middle-aged man with a cigar, who appeared to be taking everything quite leisurely, but he cut in, and for a moment gave the impression that he would hit the Rolls. He missed it.

"Damn it, I can understand his framing Cartwright, and even killing kids, but not his own—" Evans began.

A motor-cycle swept across the by-pass from the right, against the lights. Roger saw the figure astride it, a girl wearing big goggles and a crash helmet, so that she was almost unrecognisable. A police car by the cross-roads started into action. Roger jammed his foot down hard. The motor-cycle cut across the Rolls-Royce, and Maddison jammed on his brakes.

The Rolls-Royce was veering to one side; it looked as if Maddison had been so startled that he had lost control. It banged into the stone wall round the centre of the roundabout and, as it did so, the girl motor-cyclist stopped by the passenger's side of the car. The police car would not have reached her in time to stop her. Maddison was leaning back against his seat, as if dazed; the door was opened, and the girl stretched her arm inside and grabbed the case.

Roger drew alongside.

The motor-cycle was between him and the Rolls, and there was no room for the rider to get away. Case in hand, head twisted round, she looked dumbfounded. Evans was already out of the car. The police car from the other side of the road came up, and a man jumped out of it and began to regulate the traffic. Maddison's head was against the back of his seat, and his eyes were closed.

Roger saw them flicker open. For a second the girl glanced at him, then he closed his eyes again.

The girl said: "Get out of my way or I'll kill the child."

And she raised the case head-high, unfastening the catch as she did so.

She looked as if she meant exactly what she said, and there was a long pause before Roger asked: "Why don't you order her not to, Maddison?"

That was the great chance and the great moment. If he were right, and he felt sure that he was, the question would startle both Maddison and the girl long enough to give him the opportunity he needed. And he was right. The girl glanced, astounded, at Maddison. Maddison's eyes opened and he sat bolt upright. Roger simply reached up and took the case away from the girl.

Cars had stopped, a coach was drawn up nearby, more policemen had arrived; but Roger was oblivious of them all.

The girl, with her crash helmet off, answered Helen Osborn's description beyond any doubt. She was now handcuffed to a uniformed policeman who had come from a car. One line of traffic was being allowed to trickle past, and a few pedestrians were slipping across the road, to add to the confusion, until everyone moved to the wide verge at the side of the road, and more police arrived, to keep the crowd back.

Maddison looked pale and sick as he demanded: "What's been happening? Where is my baby?"

"*Whose* baby?" asked Roger coldly.

Evans exclaimed: "Good God!"

"Don't ask ridiculous questions," Maddison said. "Are you utterly mad? My own child—"

"Don't keep it up," Roger said. "This isn't your child, and you know it. It's your nephew's, I suspect. You probably hated the child from the moment you knew it was on the way, and you hated your nephew enough to try to frame him for murders he didn't commit. Those things add up nicely. You planned a way of avenging yourself on everyone – killing the child which wasn't yours, making the mother suffer without knowing that you knew, and damning your nephew. I suppose it's possible to comprehend how you felt about your wife's child, but those other babies—"

"You *are* mad!" Maddison cried. "I don't know what you're talking about."

"I can tell you about those other babies," Helen Osborn said, and it was the first time she had spoken. Her lips were curled tightly, and there was a glitter in her eyes. "He always hated the girls who would have nothing to do with him. He used to tell me so, when I lived with him." There was a note of deep bitterness in her voice. "I think his wife's child drove him round the bend. He's a psychopath – that's the truth about Ted Maddison. He couldn't have kids, so no one he had ever cared for must have them either."

Maddison was glaring at her.

"How long have you known this?" demanded Roger.

"I had an idea after the Kindle baby was killed," Helen Osborn answered. "Corrissey was behaving in a queer way, too. Corrissey would do whatever Maddison told him to. Did you know that? When I asked Corrissey what was up, he said Cartwright was on the run and the old man wanted him helped. But I wasn't fooled, and I gave Corrissey the all-clear to let Cartwright out, then took your officer along. I thought that if you had Cartwright, it would tie everything up; but Corrissey killed your man and nearly killed me."

She was talking in a low-pitched, tense voice.

"When May released you, why didn't you come straight to us?" demanded Roger.

"Because I hoped to get plenty for keeping quiet," Helen Osborn said, and her very cynicism made that sound true. "I phoned Maddison, told him what I knew, and said I'd get rid of his wife's kid and keep quiet if he'd pay me enough. But I warned the wife, didn't I? I knew you'd look after the kid if I did that. Call me bad," she added, "even call me heartless, but I wouldn't have killed the kid. Maddison's the killer."

There was nothing she would not say, now, to try to help herself.

After a long pause Roger said: "Edward Ralph Maddison, it is my duty to arrest you on a charge of complicity in the murder of James Gibson, a detective officer, at about—"

Then, as Roger finished, he heard Spendlove's voice.

"Damned nice work, Handsome. Will you let Cartwright go free now?"

"I wouldn't be surprised," Roger said. "How did you get here?"

"Didn't you know I had one unfailing recipe for success as a crime reporter?" asked Spendlove. "I find out where you're going, and follow."

Roger sat in his office early that afternoon with Evans squatting on a chair near him and Commander Hardy sitting back in the easy chair. The telephones were silent. The pile of reports on Roger's desk was high, but none had been touched since lunchtime, and then he had hardly glanced through them.

Maddison was at Cannon Row police station, and there would be a special afternoon court to hear the charge against him. Helen Osborn was in a nearby cell, and would be charged at the same time.

"I don't think we'll find we'll be able to fix the Shaw and the Kindle murders on to Maddison," Roger said. "I've checked as far as I can in the time. There isn't much doubt that Corrissey was the actual killer, and that Maddison put him up to it – he was not only utterly dominated by Maddison, but well paid by him. He was absolutely loyal, and Maddison could safely tell him anything. But after Corrissey died Maddison acted for himself.

"Corrissey probably knew about the quarrel between Cartwright and the Kindle woman, and may actually have waited for such a quarrel. But I don't think Maddison wanted his nephew caught too quickly; he assumed it would be some time before the police got on to him, and planned the other murders quickly – while Cartwright was free. Maddison was genuinely worried about Cartwright, and wanted him free, remember. An early arrest would have spoiled his plans."

"What I don't see yet is how you got on to the truth," Evans said. He talked quite naturally, none of the sullenness lingering, and Roger doubted whether he would ever again feel that inferiority complex. "What made you think the child wasn't Maddison's?"

"An itch to find out what might make Maddison our man, plus an old doctor friend," Roger said. "There was the coincidence of the mothers having worked at Maddisons, too. It looked like a psychopathic job from the beginning, but psychopaths have motives, remember. Who would have one against these different girls? Not Cartwright; he was too young, that was fairly certain. Maddison? There was at least one pointer to him – the unnatural tension of his wife, who had a guilt obsession, rather like Anne Kindle. She hated Cartwright, and I kept wondering why. His uncle was a lecher, and

Cartwright inherited his farmyard habits. Nice enough chap in other ways," Roger went on. "I don't doubt that his uncle was watching him closely, and saw a way to frame him – and make him look a psycho. Any man who killed *two* babies surely must be. Maddison probably knew about Cartwright's quarrel with Anne Kindle, and struck quickly that night. Then Cartwright realised he was being framed, and guessed why. He made his big mistake in faking a suicide to fool us, and running away to try to get the truth out of Corrissey. At the time that probably looked reasonable. Later, of course, wearing one of Cartwright's caps, Maddison attacked the Graham child. No woman who had scorned him was safe."

"Well, I'm damned," Evans said weakly.

A few days later, the general outline of the report that Roger had made to Hardy was confirmed. By then Hilda Maddison, with her child, was living in a small country hotel. The affairs of Maddison Brothers were under Cartwright's control, for better or worse, and Bert May had already been promoted to take Corrissey's place. Edward Maddison had entered a formal 'not guilty' plea at the first hearing, but the case against him was rapidly building up.

Knowing all these things and putting the finishing touches to the case, Roger went to see Ledbetter of AS Division the day before the second hearing. Ledbetter looked as tough as ever, but there was a smile in his eyes as he said: "All right, I was wrong and you were right – we all have to have the luck sometimes. I've got one piece of news that will please your romantic heart."

"What's that?'

"Anne Kindle's husband is being flown home by his company and is due tomorrow," Ledbetter answered. "Apparently that's done the young woman a power of good."

"That's one of the things I wanted to hear," Roger said.

JOHN CREASEY

GIDEON'S DAY

Gideon's day is a busy one. He balances family commitments with solving a series of seemingly unrelated crimes from which a plot nonetheless evolves and a mystery is solved.

One of the most senior officers within Scotland Yard, George Gideon's crime solving abilities are in the finest traditions of London's world famous police headquarters. His analytical brain and sense of fairness is respected by colleagues and villains alike.

'The finest of all Scotland Yard series' – New York Times.

GIDEON'S FIRE

Commander George Gideon of Scotland Yard has to deal successively with news of a mass murderer, a depraved maniac, and the deaths of a family in an arson attack on an old building south of the river. This leaves little time for the crisis developing at home ....

'Gideon of Scotland Yard emerges as one of the most real working detectives in modern fiction.... A sympathetic and believable professional policeman.' - New York Times

JOHN CREASEY

THE CREEPERS

"The prisoner's hand was thin and bony ... And in the centre of the palm was a pinkish mark. It was the shape of a wolf's head, mouth open, fangs showing. Although it was what he had expected to see, Inspector West felt a twinge of repugnance a stab not unrelated to fear. It was the fifth time he had seen the mark of the wolf – the mark of Lobo."

A gang of cat burglars led by Lobo cause mayhem as they terrorize the city. They must be stopped, but with little in the way of evidence the police are baffled. Just how can Inspector West manage to do this in what is a race against time before more victims succumb?

"Here is an excellent novel of law enforcement officers, harried, discouraged and desperately fatigued, moving inexorably ahead under the pressure of knowledge that they must succeed to save human lives." - Cleveland Plain-Dealer

"Furiously exciting" - Chicago Tribune

"The action is fast, continuous and exciting" - San Francisco News

JOHN CREASEY

THE HOUSE OF THE BEARS

Standing alone in the bleak Yorkshire Moors is Sir Rufus Marne's 'House of the Bears'. Dr. Palfrey is asked to journey there to examine an invalid - who has now disappeared. Moreover, Marne's daughter lies terribly injured after a fall from the minstrel's gallery which Dr. Palfrey discovers was no accident. He sets out to investigate and the results surprise even him . . . .

> *"'Palfrey' and his boys deserve to take their places among the immortals." - Western Mail*

INTRODUCING THE TOFF

Whilst returning home from a cricket match at his father's country home, the Honourable Richard Rollison - alias The Toff - comes across an accident which proves to be a mystery. As he delves deeper into the matter with his usual perseverance and thoroughness, murder and suspense form the backdrop to a fast moving and exciting adventure.

'The Toff has been promoted to a place of honour among amateur detectives.' – The Times Literary Supplement

Printed in Great Britain
by Amazon